TEEWAHPANYEE THE BOY, TWO FEATHERS THE MAN

Book 7

In the New Life Series

By

Louise Bouck

ACKNOWLEDGEMENTS

It is important to say thank you to all the people who have encouraged me. A special thank you goes to those who have continued in unfailing prayer support. A big thank you hug goes to my husband, Dale Bouck. He managed to keep my computer running in spite of the monsoons. Thank you for being a willing editor, Dale. Thank you to my family members that suffered through reading rough drafts. A big thank you goes to Maureen Burge. She encourages, edits and hugs. It is appreciated more than I can say.

Thank you, to Ray Shaw, who showed that special gift of patience when helping me with new technology. Without him my stories would still be files in my computer. He is amazing! Thank you to the folks in the computer lab. What would any of us do without the public libraries and the wonderful people that work there?

DEDICATION

This New Life Series is dedicated to Jesus and my family, those that have gone before me, those that are with me and those to come and to my brothers and sisters in Christ.

†

PROLOGUE

As the stories of "The New Life Series" have unfolded, of course God's blessings and provision are evident. Much has happened and many adventures have taken place, new people and new locations have added to the depth of the lives of our characters as both drama and joy have filled their days.

Book one, "More Than Survival," introduces the Slater family and shows us how a fifteen-year-old boy could survive the loss of his family and build a life from nothing in the wilderness of the new frontier.

Book two, "Life's Many Journeys," takes us along the Hickory and Silver Rivers as two young men form a lifelong brotherly bond and rescue a woman that brings love.

Book three, "The Land's Heritage" watches the development of homesteads and a settlement, as they struggle to build a lasting heritage and strong faith for the coming generation.

Book four, "The Story of Sarah," at nearly nine years old she was taken from the Slater's covered wagon. Her mind, her faith, and her strength of will and courage were tested by the Winahatah Indians. She develops many skills while planting seeds of faith. Her discovery, and her ability to see and pass on its potential, saves the people she grows to love.

Book five, "Together," brought Sarah to the arms of her brother and his family at last. She used her skills to save lives and a man from the Winahatah village found her. They returned to the people just in time.

Book six, "The Blue Stone People," is filled with the growing faith of the Indian village. After Sarah left, evil visited. A young Jesuit priest arrived to teach from the Bible, while people from the north came with a dark plan and a demon filled shaman.

Now, please enjoy book seven.

TABLE OF CONTENTS

CHAPTER ONE
RETURN TO BE BRAVE

"You must stay away for three nights, Teewah."

"Yes, Father, I know, and I have everything packed that I am allowed to take. Father, do not worry about me. I like to walk the woods alone and now that I have my horse, it will be even better. Mother insisted that I take the blanket that she made. I don't think that it is allowed, but if it will make her feel better, I will take it and put it under me on the horse and not use it to cover myself.

"Teewah, which way will you head?"

"I think north, toward the mountains, I cannot tell anyone more than that."

"Yes, son, I should not have asked. Remember that the weather can change quickly this time of year. Be sure to find a place where there is shelter or take the time to make one. If you manage to bring back game, it will be a great honor.

"Yes, Father, I will try." Teewahpanyee smiled broadly as he swung up on his brown and white paint and nodded to his mother. He had said his goodbye to her and now she bravely stood smiling in front of their tent, with her arms wrapped tightly around Tennalaylah her only daughter.

Tennalaylah laughed and waved frantically as her big brother rode slowly through the center of camp, with his head held high and his chin jutting forward, trying to be impressive. He was making sure that everyone saw him. This was a time of joy for the people. Another young man would return to be a brave warrior and hunter. They acknowledged him as he moved slowly past each tent. Some applauded, all stood and smiled, while a few friends called out his name.

"See you in three days, Teewah." His best friend Miclois had returned with a large deer. He wanted very much to do the same.

His mother however, was having difficulty imagining her young son, as a warrior, when he rode out. She had heard stories of other boys not ever returning, when they had left camp for their time alone. Three nights is such a long time, she thought as a single tear betrayed her smile and slid onto her cheek before being brushed quickly away.

She couldn't help feeling proud as she watched her handsome son, with his shining brown skin and jet-black hair. She had taken special care that morning to oil his skin and hair, pulling it back into a ridged bar on the back of his head. She had wound cords around it to hold it in place and had inserted a feather from a spotted owl that he had brought to her one morning after wandering in the woods. He looks much like his father today, she thought, but he is still a boy. Thirteen years old is not a man, she thought, as she turned and ducked into her tent.

Only last night she had finished placing the shells and bone beads on the spirit pouch that he now wore around his neck. She had carefully rolled hairs, one from her head, his father's and sister's into a small ball of clay mud and placed it near the fire to bake. This bead was the first item to go into his spirit bag. It would keep a part of his family close to his heart always.

Although it was not a boisterous celebration, everyone was excited. Their Shaman, Night Crier, had painted signs on the front shoulders of Teewahpanyee's pony and more on the flanks. These were intended to ward off evil and to protect him.

Teewah was glad when he was out of camp and as soon as he left the last tent behind, he urged his mount to a canter and then a full gallop as they headed for the woods. All eyes followed him until he was in the trees and out of sight.

When he was sure that they could no longer see him, he slowed and then finally stopped at the little stream that was the camp's water supply; to fill his water bag. Dismounting, he patted his horse and talked to her.

"We are about to have an adventure, my friend. See what I have hidden in the rocks for you. Teewah uncovered a pouch of wild grain that he had picked. I may find myself hungry, but you will not be. I promise that I will always take good care of you."

He moved on, and Teewah followed the stream, as it grew ever so slightly larger, meandering through the trees heading north to the distant mountains.

"I must be cautious, since the ground shaking, trees may be unstable." They had felt the quake but no damage had been detected in their camp.

That night, Teewah slept beside the flowing water, imagining what it would be like to return to the village with a deer or perhaps even a bear. He could hear the imaginary cheers of the people as their Chief gave him a new name. He could almost feel the heat of the communal fire that the people would gather around to honor him. There would be a feast and dancing and all the maidens would look at him with admiration, hoping for some attention from him. His mother would serve him his food as she did his father. He would never again be expected to do the chores of a child.

"See my friend; we have spent our first night in the woods alone with no trouble. Let us be on our way." He swung up and settled on the beautiful blanket his mother had insisted that he take with him.

"Soon I will see the tracks of a large animal, and we will follow it. I wish to return with honor," he said nudging the horse forward with his heels.

When he crossed the tracks of a large cat, he continued on without following its path. I want an animal that is meat, he thought, but it is good that I know I am in a cat's territory. I must be careful.

Teewah stopped to rest his horse and drink from the stream that had doubled in size.

"Here my friend, would you like some grain?" He offered the wide-open pouch to the horse.

Teewah was allowed to drink water, but he was not to eat anything unless he had hunted it. He laughed at how simple it would be to cheat. I didn't, but I could have stashed food for myself as well as my horse, but this is a test of honor, he thought. I would never do that. He crept slowly and silently along the edge of the water, looking for a trail with many little prints. He had hunted small game often. When he found a path, it was easy for him to get one of the rabbits that had made the prints. Soon he had a small fire going and a rabbit roasting on a branch.

The mountains are much farther than I thought. It will take another day or more of riding to reach the foothills. I can't go that far this time. Tonight will be my second night. I must move closer to camp tomorrow and search for game as I go. I want to enter camp the morning of the fourth day with a large animal. It was at that moment that he turned slowly, to look in the direction of the sunset. There among the brush was a deer. It isn't a large deer, but it is meat. I must accept what the spirits have brought to me. He raised his bow and the arrow flew through the brush, careening off of a branch as the deer, bounded away unharmed.

Teewah was disgusted with himself, as he searched for his arrow and placed it back in his quiver. That is what I get for not concentrating, or perhaps for thinking that the deer was small. The spirits are angry with me. What should I do to show them I am sorry? The Shaman paints his face before talking to the spirits. That is what I should do, he thought.

Teewah added ash from his small fire to several drops of water in his palm and mixed it until it became a black paste. He drew a line across each cheek and just for good measure; he added two bars going down his chin. He would never have admitted it, but he was having fun. His reflection in the rippling water was unrecognizable. This ought to make the spirits listen to me when I speak, he thought.

Kneeling by the fire with up-lifted hands, he began to chant, sounds he had heard all his life, but didn't have a full understanding of their meaning.

"Spirits of the night wind, I ask your forgiveness," he spoke loudly, making his voice deeper, as if volume or depth gave him authority. The deer you sent for me was a fine deer. I hurried my shot and nearly lost my arrow. If you will send another deer in the morning, I promise I will shoot carefully and accurately."

A loud clap of thunder startled him. He stood up and looked around. His heart was pounding hard as he considered whether the sound had been a reply to his appeal. Another rumble seemed to be directly above him, and then a loud bang sent sparks and fire danced down the length of the tallest tree, near him. It started a small fire in the brush at its base. Teewah, hurried to put it out, stomping and dumping his water bag and running to refill it and dump it again and again until the fire had finally sputtered out.

It was then that he recalled his father's advice, "Be sure to find a place with shelter." He had not thought of it, but now he wished that he had, as the rain began to fall. I can't travel in the dark; my pony might get hurt. Besides how would I find shelter? I can't see anything but my fire and it is getting smaller. Teewah sat back down near the fire and added wood, but he got more smoke than flame. The rain is making all the wood wet, he thought.

He was sure that the rain was caused by the spirits to show him they were unhappy. He pulled a few bites from the rabbit, but somehow he just didn't feel hungry anymore. If I don't change my ways, I will fail.

"Spirits, will you forgive me and please help me?" His voice was no longer loud and didn't sound like he was trying to be impressive.

As Teewah lay wet and tired near the fire, a huge golden mountain lion moved slowly toward him, out of the darkness. Its muscles rippled as it walked, swinging its tail back and forth in gentle rhythm to each step. It sat down across the small fire pit facing him, as if it were a Chief at a council meeting. Teewah froze; holding his breath until he felt his lungs would burst.

As the lion locked eyes with Teewah, it spoke and the sound of its words bounced off the trees, shattering the sound of the rain on the leaves of the forest.

"Teewahpanyee, you must return to your village. You are needed there. Do not fear. I will be with you." The huge lion stood and turned, flicking its tail, causing a small clump of its hair to float in the air toward Teewah, as it moved into the darkness.

Early morning found Teewah curled in a small ball, lying close to the smoldering embers. His face paint was smeared in a layer covering most of his face. As he rubbed his eyes, the ash stung them.

With both hands he splashed the cold water of the stream onto his face and rubbed until he felt the ash paint was gone. He peered once again at his reflection, but couldn't tell if his face was totally clean. He shook his head trying to clear it of the sharp image it held of the huge lion.

"Teewahpanyee, you are a stupid fool. You were to learn to be a man. So far all you have done is behave like an irresponsible child. You missed the deer. You didn't build a shelter, and now you are having bad dreams." He scolded himself out loud as he walked to the fire to be sure it was out.

As he knelt to stir the embers, he noticed the small tuft of golden hair, snagged on one of the rocks that he had placed around his fire. Immediately he was able to remember the entire scene clearly, the huge mountain lion and its strange message. With reverence, he picked up the strands of soft hair and carefully tucked them in his spirit bag.

Attentively he circled the fire, expecting to see big cat prints in the wet ground. There were none.

When he looked up at his pony, he saw that the symbols that the shaman had painted were still intact. They hadn't washed away in the rain. He patted the horse and slid his finger softly over the design on its flank of a lions paw, feeling a slight shiver as he did.

"We must head back, my friend." If I see game on the way I will get it, but I must hurry back. Suddenly, I have awareness that something is very wrong in the village. Why would they need me? I can see the village from the edge of the woods and if it looks peaceful and everything seems normal, I will stay in the woods tonight and return as planned in the morning. I cannot get that lion out of my head. What did he mean? I will be with you.

Teewah's thoughts kept him distracted as he rode along. His horse slowed and quietly stopped, at the edge of a clearing.

There, feeding in the grass not faraway was a very large buck. Teewah held his breath, drawing his bow carefully. He released his arrow before getting down. The large deer was his.

"Thank you for giving me your life, to bring food to my village," he said, as he slid from his horse.

As soon as the deer was prepared and lashed to a travois, he was on his way again. He wasted no time.

Both his mind and heart told him that the message he had received during the night was authentic. He was sure of it. He couldn't remember ever seeing that clearing in the woods, and why did my horse ease up so quietly. Surely the spirits are here with me, helping me, but I don't know why they would. I must hurry. Teewah felt an increasing urgency to return to his village. He could smell smoke.

Teewah stopped and climbed the tallest tree in the area. He could see a large smudge of smoke in the sky, in the direction of the village. It is too much smoke to be cooking fires. What has happened? He was worried as he scurried down and jumped on his horse, on the run. He was concerned and anxious but he rode through the trees skillfully, being sure that his path would not cause the travois to snag. He knew he had to be cautious to protect his mount from harm. He could only think of one thing that might make that much smoke. Someone must have died. It must be smoke from a funeral pyre.

As he burst from the trees at a gallop, he reigned in his horse and abruptly stopped. He couldn't grasp what he was seeing. Every tent in the village of the Sentu had been burned. People lay in unnatural positions on the ground, exhibiting wounds and broken bones. Arrows pierced them, or gun shots brought pools of blood where they lay. The village was silent.

Teewahpanyee ran to the remains of his parent's tent in sorrow. In the smoldering circle lay his mother and sister's bodies. His father had defended them a few feet in front of it until he fell to an arrow of the raiders. A scream crept from the depth of his soul and exploded from his mouth, as he knelt and wept.

When Teewah had no more tears to give, he slowly rose, looking around, wondering what he should do. The scene was overwhelming. Everything and everyone that he had ever known and loved were gone.

As he stood there dazed and numb, he heard a sob. Standing still, he listened and turned in the direction of the sound. The very small stream he had followed in the woods meandered along a path behind the camp. There in the tall weeds and brush willow, he found a young girl, holding a chubby baby boy. Gently he lifted the boy from her arms and helped her up.

"They are gone. They will not come back." It was the only comfort he could offer her. She stood beside him, still sobbing, until the boy began to cry, too. Reaching for the baby, she turned her attention to him and was able to gain her composure.

"He is hungry. He hasn't eaten since yesterday. When they came, I ran and jumped into the water behind the bushes. Water Bug was already there. His mother let him play in the water when she was working nearby. They took his mother and my cousin, too."

"Who did this? Who were they?"

"I do not know them. They wore strange paint on their faces and their hair stood up on top of their heads, each with tall reeds and feathers in it. The hair on their horses stood in spikes on their heads and they had turned the horse's tails into brushes."

Teewah suddenly realized that not only did he have the people of their entire village to send to the spirit world; he had this fragile looking girl and hungry baby to care for. How could he do it? His hand sought his spirit bag. He silently sought aid. Spirit lion, if you are really here with me. Show me what I am to do.

He turned quickly and led his horse away from camp, back to the edge of the trees on the other side of the stream. He motioned for her to follow.

Clearing a circle in the sod, he started a fire and hung a large chunk from his deer, over it to roast.

Efficiently, he moved, creating a shelter from branches. After spreading the blanket his mother had made, on the grass, he asked her to sit. He felt ashamed at his failure to build a shelter to keep it dry. The blanket had shrunk and the colors of the wool had bled into each other. The baby continued to wail. He noticed then, that the girl's hands trembled as she tried to comfort the child. Teewah looked at her with compassion, aware of what she had seen and heard.

"When were they here?" he asked softly.

"They rode out of the morning sun. No one saw them until they were here."

"If I take the boy, do you think you could find us something to use to cook grain? I have some in my bag. Perhaps, he would eat it, if it is cooked soft enough."

She transferred the boy to Teewah's arms and walked hesitantly back toward camp and the horrible scene that existed there. She grabbed the first two pots that she found and ran with them to the stream, cleaning them and filling them each with water. She returned quickly, offering first Teewah and then the baby a drink from the larger one and placed the smaller on the fire to heat.

"I will be back," she said, this time running. She dashed here and there picking up a cup here and a bone spoon there, another small pot and a deer hide that had not been burned, because it was still stretched in the grass, where someone had been working it. She pretended she could not see anything else.

Once again she returned, placing the things she had collected near the fire. Teewah looked at her with respect. She has been through so much, but still she tries to serve others. I don't even know her name.

18

"Tell me, what is your name?"

"I do not wish to say my name, just as I do not say the name of the dead in camp. My heart is dead, although my body moves and my hands work."

"I accept that," said Teewah. "We should take new names. I will call you, Willow, because the willow sheltered you near the water and shielded you from their sight."

"We can call the boy, Water Bug," she offered. "That is just a name I gave him. It is not his real name. I have seen his mother pick him out of the water many times. He loves the water. What about you? What should we call you?"

Teewah shook his head, but didn't answer. He poured the grain he had picked for his horse, into the boiling water and walked back to the still-smoldering village. He wandered about looking for a sign, or direction.

"Spirit lion, what name would you have me take?" As he spoke, he noticed that two eagle feathers lay on the ground at his feet. He picked them up and brushed them clean of dust. His people considered the eagle sacred. He wondered where they had come from. Just then, he heard the cry of an eagle as it sailed overhead and disappeared above the clouds.

Teewah returned to his small shelter without looking left or right. As he looked up at Willow, he saw that she had quieted the boy, by giving him an outer edge piece of deer meat to chew on. She stirred the grain.

"It is nearly soft enough. He has some teeth. I think he will be able to eat what we do, if we give him small soft bites."

19

"That is good. After you feed him, I think he will sleep. He looks very tired."

Willow spooned bites of the soft grain into the boy's mouth and he seemed happy with it. Soon he cuddled near her sucking his thumb and in another minute or two, he was sound asleep.

Teewah cut a piece of meat and handed it to Willow and a second for himself.

"We must eat. At first light tomorrow we will begin to do what needs to be done. It will be overwhelmingly, dreadful work, but there is no one else to do it."

"Yes," she said. "We must."

CHAPTER TWO
WORK AS A TEAM

The early light of dawn found Teewahpanyee awake. He had walked softly away between the trees. A large brown horse from the village herd had come back to graze nearby. He searched the area and found two others in the trees. Teewah placed a short rope on each and led them back near the shelter before hobbling them. They would be able to freely wander the area to graze and drink. It simply would keep them from running.

Willow had cried out in her sleep during the night and Teewah felt sure that today's tasks would add to her nightmares. When she was up, they gently woke Water Bug and cleaned and fed him.

"What will we do with him while we are working? I don't want him in the water or near the village or our campfire," he said.

"Some of the mothers put their babies in a harness and let them sit on the back of a gentle horse as it grazes. We could try to make a harness that would keep him safe and put him on the tan mare that you brought back. She is very gentle. I know her."

Together they figured out a way to keep the baby safely on the horse. When they looked back at him he was laughing and swinging his arms. Willow walked resolutely beside Teewah as he led the big brown horse into the woods.

"We need to make two huge piles of wood in the center of camp. There are several dead trees on that hill just ahead. I am hoping that we can pull them, one at a time, to the center of camp."

21

Willow helped all she could, by tying ropes to thick branches and passing them back to Teewah as he fastened them to the saddle horn.

"This horse must have belonged to one of our top warriors. Most of our men didn't use a saddle. He must have obtained it in a battle or raid. It helps to have something to tie the ropes to."

When they had used all the rope they could find, they decided to try to move the tree. The horse strained, trying his best to do what Teewah asked of him. Slowly the tree slid a few feet and then snagged.

In time, they found a path through the trees and brush and were able to get the dead tree to the center of camp. The next tree was not as difficult. They had learned how to do it and the best path to take. A third and a forth would be needed to keep the fires burning.

With the wood in place, Teewah instructed Willow to walk with him so that they could work together.

"You need to help me place our people on the wood. I can't do it alone. I wish I could."

"I know. I will help all that I can, but it seems wrong to not wrap them."

"We would, Willow, if we could, but all the blankets and furs are burned. Neither of us wants to do this, but out of respect for our people we must. I wish to start at the tent of my family," he said. "Do you think it would be wrong if we take one thing from each person as we do this? Our people are gone, but they will not be forgotten."

"It is a good thing. We will remember them and teach Water Bug about his people, the Sentu."

A basket of shells had burned leaving only a pile of ash and shells near his mother. He touched the beautiful work on his spirit bag, and picked up one of the tiny shells and slipped it inside his pouch. He lifted his little sister in his arms and walked to the pile of wood alone. When he gently laid her down he rolled her on her side and with his knife, he cut a lock of the silky black hair from the back of her head where the flames had not reached. He coiled it around his finger, and this too, he placed in the pouch.

As he knelt beside his father, he lifted a bear claw necklace and placed it around his own neck.   With much effort, together, they were able to place him beside his daughter and wife.

The next tent had belonged to one of the braves and his wife. The warrior had dropped near Teewah's father. Teewah removed a fire horn and slipped it onto Willow's belt. His wife had decorated many shirts and had worked with bone beads and furs. Willow had watched her and studied the way she had made the intricate patterns that decorated some of the most prized clothing in the village. The furs were burned but a pile of bone beads lay among the ashes. Willow picked each one up and tucked them securely into her pocket. One day I will use them and remember you.

The next tent was that of their Chief. He was wise, old, and loved. His people had honored him. Near the tent, his clay pipe lay broken and useless. Teewah picked it up. He looked at Willow for approval. It was considered a sacred thing. She nodded as he pushed the pieces into his deep shirt pocket. It was then, that they both realized that the Chief's body was not there. They looked throughout the village with no success.

"They have taken him with evil intent. It is a sad thing that we have not found him. It would be better if we had." His voice was so soft and tormented that it reached to Willow's heart like nothing else had. She forced her words to match his.

"We must move on."

The ritual of choosing a memento for each person was continued. There were sixty-two families living in the village at the time of the raid. Willow silently pulled a silver comb from her mother's hair. Teewah picked up a knife that lay near her father. He handed it to her.

"This is from your father. It will serve you well." She bit her lip until she tasted blood, trying not to sob, but it was impossible to stifle the emotions they were feeling. Father God, help me. She prayed silently. Roughly they scrubbed away tears, leaving black smudges of ash on their cheeks as they worked to finish the task of creating the funeral pyres they could not have imagined. They were living a nightmare that would never completely leave either of them.

It was late in the afternoon when they lit the two fires in the center of what had been their village.

"I cannot offer a ceremony as our shaman would have, but I make this simple request. Good spirits of the next world, take our people where they will be happy. Help them on their way," he said.

Teewah looked over at Willow as she stared at the awful flames consuming the last hope of ever again looking on the faces of the people. Tears streamed down her face washing streaks in the black. Her prayer broke the silence.

"Father, be merciful to our people. Most of them did not know you, but they believed in a Great Spirit that created them. Take them to be happy with you in heaven. My mother tried to plant seeds of faith, and my father was beginning to believe. Please receive them."

"Tomorrow we will search again for anything that might be useful, but we have done all we can today." Teewah placed his arm around Willow's shoulders protectively as they walked toward the tan mare. She had stayed close to the temporary shelter all day. Teewah lifted the baby down and Willow took him to the water to clean him and allow him to splash and play, while Teewah warmed the cooked grain. They had been vaguely aware of his crying midday when he had tired of his place on the horse. He was hungry and wanted down. Finally he had cried himself to sleep.

Willow scrubbed her hands, arms, and face, arms again and legs, and feet but she couldn't rid herself of the strong smell of the funeral fire and death.

When Willow brought Water Bug back to their little shelter, she saw that Teewah had cut a large bundle of branches and was busy lashing them together. "We must dry the meat of this deer or it will be useless soon." He had another piece of meat cooking over the fire and had placed bits of the cooked roast in the pot with the grain.

Later, as the baby slept, they sliced the meat, putting it on the racks he had made.

"Teewahpanyee, you gave me a new name and we agreed on Water bug, for the boy, but what will your new name be?"

"Our people are no more. We must be a new people with new ways, and new names, "he replied.

When I walked in the camp yesterday, these blew near my feet." He pulled the two eagle feathers from his pocket, gently smoothing them. Being in his pocket was damaging them.

"I wish to be called Two Feathers."

"That is a good name," she said, placing the feathers inside a large pot.

"We will be called the people of the Spirit Lion," he stated it as an accepted fact.

"Yes," she agreed, "He is the most powerful Lion of Judah, and Son of the Living God."

"What is this that you are talking about?"

"Oh Two Feathers, Lion of Judah, is a name for Jesus."

"I still do not understand. Who is this Jesus, and how do you know of these things?"

"I learned them from my mother. She came on a boat from very far away, with her husband to teach people about Jesus. Her husband was killed, and the braves brought her here. My father bought her for four horses. She was very beautiful and knew about many important things."

"Yes, she was beautiful. I remember her well. Let me think on this, for I saw the Spirit Lion on my vision quest. He sent me back to the village early and told me I was needed. Perhaps I will hear more of it another time. Now you should rest."

"Sleep well, Two Feathers," She said, as she curled up on the edge of the blanket next to the little boy. Every part of her hurt, both her body and spirit felt as if it had been beaten and broken. Her arms ached from the long day of lugging wood and bodies to the pyres and then slicing the meat for drying.

26

Two Feathers was puzzled by what Willow had said earlier. It is not right that a girl should know things that I have not heard.

Tomorrow I will hear more of this Lion of Judah. His mind was busy as he walked to the center of the village to add more wood to the two huge fires that burned there.

When he returned, he added wood to their campfire. He wanted it to continue burning brightly for two reasons. The meat needed to dry to be preserved, but also, he knew that the fire offered protection. Wild animals would not come near their fires.

"Great Lion Spirit, what am I to do with this girl and baby? She is not much more than a child and yet she speaks with knowledge and seems wise. Did you hurry me back to camp because of them? Are we to stay here or to move on?

The men's council at the summer meeting spoke of the land to the south. They said that it is warmer there and that snow does not reach there. Should I take them and go far to the south? What of the corn that is growing? It is not ready yet. If we leave it, later we will wish we had it to eat. If we stay to harvest it, it will be late in the year. We will not get far before the cold of winter comes. I don't know what to do." He too was in agony on many levels. Responsibility rested heavily on his sore shoulders.

Two Feathers stretched out on the grass near the shelter and watched the smoke from the fires drift up covering some of the stars. The three-quarter moon cast a blue glow on the willows and brush along the little stream. If we stay here, we know that we will have water and the ground here grows the corn. The deer are plentiful, and at least now I know that if I concentrate, I can bring one back when I see one. We would not starve here. We have two hides and I can get more so we can make a tent. With that comforting thought, Two Feathers finally fell asleep.

Willow was adding wood to their campfire when he opened his eyes.

"Rest for a little longer, Two Feathers. I have added enough wood to keep the village fires burning and I want to go to the stream to bathe before we begin our work today. I am hoping that Water Bug will sleep a little longer." She walked quietly away.

The sky in the east was softly turning a pale yellow along the edge of the earth, when Willow returned with her skirt gathered in front of her; she was carrying food to prepare for their meal. She had picked some corn and pulled cattail roots along the stream. Placing them near the fire, she picked up the pot containing the grain and meat mash and walked to the open grassland, picking seeds that she knew were good to eat and dropping them in the pot as she went. The tan mare approached her and rubbed its muzzle on her shoulder.

"Hello, sweet horse. How are you this morning? Are you willing to do babysitting again today, while we work? You seem disturbed by all that has happened. You do not understand where all the people have gone and the big fires probably frighten you. Don't worry. I will take you with me if we leave." Willow stood scratching the ears of the old mare and the tears came, undetected at first. I wonder if I will be able to do all that I should for Two Feathers and Water Bug. There are so many things that I don't know how to do. I was just learning how to weave. My cooking isn't that good, and I have never done any sewing.

"Jesus, please help us. I know that Two Feathers doesn't know you yet, but I will teach him all that I can." Willow dipped the pot into the stream carefully adding water without losing the grain she had picked.

When she returned to the shelter, Water Bug was up, toddling around and Two Feathers had been caring for him.

"Good Morning, my little Bug, how are you today? After we feed him, he will have to go back up on the mare again for a while. I doubt if our work today will take as long. We will need something to carry the things we should save. I wish we had a big, strong basket."

Two Feathers looked at her with a strange expression.

"I have never watched the women do their weaving. I cannot make a basket. Can you?" He asked.

"I was just starting to learn. That is something that I will have to practice later on, but it isn't a solution for right now."

"We can use one of the hides and fold up the sides. If we are careful, nothing will drop out," he suggested.

"That will have to do. We have nothing else."

Water Bug was fed, clean and placed securely on the mare in his harness. Willow and Two Feathers, worked their way through the camp, from one burned tent to the next, salvaging the items they could. It was awful to work in the horrendous devastation, but it was necessary if they were to survive. They had decided to collect anything that wasn't ruined.

"We will use what we need and perhaps we can trade the rest later on."

"That sounds as if you are sure we will leave." Willow was frowning. The thought of leaving made the loss of her family very final. She knew that they were gone, but she was young and not ready to let go of what was familiar, even though it was filled with torturous memories.

"We won't leave unless we both feel that it is the right thing to do. Willow, I won't force you to do anything that you do not want to do."

"Thank you," she said softly.

It was then that Two Feathers realized that Willow was as frightened of the future as she was horrified by the recent past. No wonder she is hesitant to follow me, she doesn't know how I will treat her or how we will survive.

"Willow, I know so little about you. How old are you?"

"I will be thirteen soon. How old are you?"

"Thirteen. I was on my vision quest. That deer is the only one I have ever shot. Willow, I know that it is hard for you to trust me. I am young and I too, have things that I haven't learned. With you it is making baskets and skill for caring for your family, but for me it is how to protect a family and provide for them. Willow, I want you to know that I will do my best to learn quickly."

"I want to make the same promise to you, Two Feathers. If you will do what you can for us, I will try to learn how to cook better and to sew and weave and all the things that are needed. I will be your sister and a mother to Water Bug. We are all that is left of our people. We will be a family."

30

"It is good that we can talk and express how we are feeling. That is what families do," he said with a small smile.

They continued to make trips to the shelter to empty the hide and check on Water Bug. He was napping, the occasional step of the horse as it grazed, rocked him gently.

"He is a good boy," she whispered. Two Feathers nodded agreement.

As they worked their way around the camp, they found one more hide that had been stretched to work. It was very stiff.

"Is this of any use?" he asked.

"I am not sure, but let's take it back with us. Look there is a large cooking pot. We will use that."

Willow was in front of her family's tent. She had not realized it immediately with things so changed. Two Feathers saw something glint in the dust near the ring of ash that had been her tent. He picked it up. A small silver cross, swung back and forth on a silver chain in his fingers. Willow's face turned gray when she saw it.

"That was my mother's. She always wore it." Two Feathers examined it carefully.

"The chain has been pulled apart, but it is intact. I will fix it for you." He placed it in her pocket carefully, making sure that it was firmly in the bottom where it would stay.

They walked swiftly up the other side of the camp. The raiders had gone back through that area. They had broken or burned everything. There was nothing to salvage.

After adding more wood to the two huge fires, they returned to their campfire to feed it, and sort what they had gathered. Willow placed all the pots near their little fire and discovered that they had seven. The stiff hide was placed with the other two on the grass.

"What can we do with these? They are all getting hard?" She asked.

Two Feathers had never been required to do it, but he knew that hides had to be scraped and rubbed with fat to soften and preserve them.

"We need to scrape all of them including my fresh hide from the deer and then rub some fat onto them. I think it is the scraping that makes them soft."

"If you will work with these, I will take Water Bug to the stream and let him enjoy the water while I try to soften this hard one," she said.

She dropped the ears of corn she had picked in the early morning, into one of the pots and poured water in it. The kernels were getting wrinkles.

"Next time I won't pick them until I am ready to cook," she said.

Water Bug was still on the back of the mare and he was fussing. He needed to be cleaned and fed. Willow pulled him down. It was hard for her. At nearly two, he was getting heavy. With the hide dragging along on one side, she led the toddler by his hand to the water. He was delighted to sit with his bare bottom in the shallow water, splashing, while she squeezed water out of the hide, trying to soften it enough to make it workable. With it spread on the grass near Water Bug, she began to scrape the soggy hide with the edge of a sharp stone as she had seen her mother do.

When she saw a tiny turtle swim over to a rock and crawl up, she picked it up and took it to Water Bug.

"This is a turtle." She said, as she placed it on his knee. The baby giggled and grabbed it. The turtle turned its head and bit the little finger that it could reach. He began to wail.

"Hush boy, you are not hurt, it was only a pinch. See, your finger is fine." She rubbed it gently and handed him a smooth stone, which he plopped into the water making a little splash.

"Let's take you back and give you some food now and put your shirt back on. Your skin is hot. I don't want you to burn." She chatted with him as she carried him back to the blanket and got him dressed.

Two Feathers had placed the corn where it could cook slowly and it was done. He fished out a small ear to cool for the boy, and cut him a thin piece of meat to gnaw on. When the opportunity presented itself, Willow spooned in a bit of mashed grain now and then. He seemed content with whatever he was given.

With corn in one hand and meat in the other, Water Bug looked up at Two Feathers and tried to talk with his mouth full of food.

"Turdall."

"Did he just say turtle?"

"Yes, I think he did. I showed him a turtle at the stream and he grabbed it. It bit his finger and I guess it made quite an impression."

"Turtle, Water Bug. You saw a turtle. Didn't you?

"Turdall," the boy smiled and mumbled smiling.

Willow leaned over and looked through the few remaining items that they had gathered. "This is a hair clip, Two Feathers. Let me show you. Give me the two feathers that you found." carefully, he removed them from the large pot where Willow had placed them for safe keeping. Willow forced the ends of the feathers down into holes that had been drilled in the piece of bone. Gently she preened the feathers. The bottom half of the bone tube had hooks carved in it. She pushed the clip firmly into the bar of hair at the back of his head.

"Thank you, Willow."

CHAPTER THREE
MAN'S WORK, WOMAN'S WORK

As the days passed, it seemed that they were in a holding pattern. Finally the two big fires in the center of camp had been allowed to burn themselves out. All that was left was bones and black ash. The next morning as Willow got up; she realized that Two Feathers was up. She saw him in the middle of the village digging a hole big enough to bury all the bones of the people. The ground was hard and the shovel he had made was not the best of tools. She fed Water Bug and got him comfortably settled on the mare before walking over to help.

"Go back, I don't want you here. This is man's work. I will do it." After he saw her turn and walk slowly back to the shelter, he felt terrible for snapping at her. What is the matter with me? Couldn't I tell her nicely? When I go back I will apologize.

Willow led the mare to the shade, where the stream entered the trees and tied her there. She could graze and drink and Water Bug would not be in the sun. When she looked up, she saw movement in the distance, between the trees. I think I see more of the horses from our village. She picked up a length of rope and walked slowly in that direction. Two horses, one brown with black mane and tail and one all brown, were grazing near the stream. She spoke softly to them, almost cooing. They raised their heads and moved slowly away from her.

"Jesus, we will need these horses. Help me to catch them. They don't know me." She tried again, this time firmly clacking her tongue and calling them, as she had

35

seen the men do, when they pulled their favorite horse from the herd. It worked and before long she had managed to fasten an end of the rope around each horse's neck. Holding on in the middle, she led them back to the shelter and fastened them to a tree.

When Two Feathers finished, he had sifted through all the ashes of both fires and had buried every bone. His entire body was covered with black ashes and he was exhausted. It was the middle of the afternoon when he walked up to the shelter where Water Bug slept and Willow was sitting in the shade trying hard to weave a simple mat. He spoke quietly.

"Willow, I am sorry that I spoke that way to you. I know that you were coming to help me. I just didn't want you to have to do that."

"I understand, Two Feathers. Let it be forgotten. You must be very tired and hungry. Please go wash and then we can eat."

Two Feathers headed for the trees beside the shelter. That is when he noticed the two horses she had tied there. "Did you find these today? I don't remember them from our herd."

"They were back in the trees. At first they wouldn't come to me."

"I will hobble them when I come back." He turned to follow the stream through the trees, but she stopped him.

"Wait just a moment. I will take the feathers and wrapping from your hair. It will be easier for me than for you."

When he returned, he had scrubbed his hair and body clean and felt much better. He had many black smudges on his leather trousers, and his long black hair lay on his back nearly to his waist. Willow wondered what his reaction would be when she told him that she could not put it back into a bar the way it had always been worn by the men of the Sentu.

Two Feathers had always been exceptionally good with horses. He rubbed their muzzles to give them his scent and scratched their ears. They seemed to sense that he would not hurt them.

As he pressed his cheek against the side of their faces and talked to them softly, he received the same response from each, a soft knicker and nod of their head. Two feathers hobbled them before turning them loose to graze the wild grain of the area.

As he walked away they followed him to the grass near the shelter. Just that quickly, they were his friend.

Willow was amazed at what she had observed. She had worked very hard to get near the horses and bring them back. How could he gain their trust so easily? She wondered.

After eating, they sat playing with Water Bug and watching the sky grow darker with heavy clouds.

"It looks like it will rain soon. I think I should gather some branches and make us a better roof on our shelter."

Two Feathers built sides with big leafy branches, fastening them tightly together. He extended the roof out another two feet and created an overhang in front.

"There, that should help to keep us dry," he said, as he sat down on the blanket beside Water Bug. While he had worked at that, Willow had gathered the meat onto a hide and covered it with another, to keep it dry. She had collected large egg-shaped stones, sticks and a thick bowl and placed them where Water Bug could play with them. She had found a gourd when they had retrieved the items from camp and it had become his favorite toy. He loved to shake it and hear it rattle. Her intention was to make a dipper, but this was a good use for it until he tired of it.

Soon a rumble of thunder warned that the storm was coming closer and Water Bug's eyes grew wide with fear at the sound. He crawled up on Willow's lap and clung to her.

"It is thunder, little one. It is going to rain. You like water and you will like the rain. Look, see the drops on my hand?" She extended her hand out again and brought it in all wet. The baby patted her hand and smiled.

"Water, rain, say rain, Water Bug."

"Rain," the baby repeated. "Rain, Rain," he said smiling and reaching for the streams of water pouring off the branches of the roof.

"Yes, rain." She said. "I wonder just how much talking he was doing before all this happened. He seems to pick up words easily."

"After this rain, the corn will fill in its kernels." Two Feathers was trying to talk optimistically. "We will have a good harvest. It will take a few weeks after this rain for it to dry and then we can pick it and it will keep. After that, we can leave if we choose. This rain will wash away some of the ash in the camp, too."

"Yes," was her only reply. She still was torn about leaving and didn't want to discuss it. He, on the other hand, was beginning to get eager to move on. He had decided that if they moved south, a little at a time, they would eventually come to a place they really liked.

They watched the rain pour down in silence for a while, each lost in their own thoughts.

Two Feathers began to make a list in his mind of the obstacles that might present themselves along the way. I know we will be vulnerable, if we meet people like the raiders that came here. Our food could spoil if it gets wet. We wouldn't want mold on our meat or corn. I wonder how hard it would be to travel with the boy. He likes to move about, but he also likes to sit on the tan mare in his harness. Maybe we should take a short trip to see how it goes and give us a break from the camp.

"Willow, did you have success with your weaving you were working on? What were you making?"

"I wouldn't call it success exactly, but I was able to make a small mat. I haven't figured out how to finish it off so it won't unravel yet." She picked up her work and offered it to him for his approval.

"That is good. If you continue to work, soon you will learn to make many useful things."

"I wish I had been more interested when I had someone to teach me." Her voice had grown husky with painful emotion.

"All my mother's beautiful baskets and mats are burned. Oh, Two Feathers, I miss my parents!" she wailed. He was at a loss to know how to comfort her. She began to cry loudly lamenting, giving voice to her grief. It was then that he realized that they had not allowed themselves time to mourn the loss of their families.

He picked up Water Bug and stepped out into the falling rain. The baby laughed and patted his hands together as they both became soaked. Two Feathers had not wanted her to see that his face had already been wet with a flood of tears that matched hers. He walked away quickly, into the woods.

"How long will it be before I can think of my family without this pain?" He cried out to the trees. Two Feathers moved swiftly through the trees and ducked under the thick branches of an old pine. It was damp there but the rain could not fully penetrate. Water Bug looked at him fearfully and began to fuss. Two Feathers rocked him and soon he was sucking his thumb quietly resting his head against the wet chest of the boy-man that held him.

As predicted, the corn grew full and the days of early fall became hot and dry. Willow had practiced weaving for hours each day and soon she had developed a pattern that was tight enough to use for containers. She folded her long mat in the middle and was able to stitch up the sides, with a cord made of cattail fibers, using a bone needle that Two Feathers made for her. She knew that her needle was a treasure. They gathered the abundant wild grains and stitched the containers shut.

One day when she was out gathering, with Water Bug toddling around near her, she could smell a familiar scent. The boy had unknowingly walked through a patch of wild mint. She was so excited that she called Two Feathers.

"Come see what Water Bug has found for us."

Two Feathers knew that she had discovered mint before he saw it. The air was delicious with it.

"We will have mint tea this winter!" He helped her pack her container full.

"Willow, you do so well with everything. I just wanted to say that I appreciate it. I know how hard it is for you to do all the things you do."

"Two Feathers, we have both worked hard and we will have to continue to do so, if we are to survive the cold months ahead."

"Willow, I think we should take the horses, and head south as soon as the corn is dried. I can watch for game along the way and we are sure to find somewhere that will be more sheltered. If I can get us some more hides, we will have enough for a tent."

"Two Feathers, that is not all that we will need. We have no winter clothes. They were all burned. How can we possibly get what we need before it is winter?"

"We must leave here, Willow. There is nothing here for us now but the bones of our people and the blackened earth they rest in. Tell me that you will go with me."

"I will go," she said sadly.

"Good, then it is settled. We will both work hard to make as many storage pouches as we can, for the meat and the corn. I can learn to weave too, if you will show me."

"Two Feathers, how will we keep the rain out of the pouches? It will ruin the food."

"I will think on it," he said as he removed the hobble and swung up on his pony, Patches. I need to hunt. Will you be alright until I return?"

"Yes, I will gather great piles of the tall grass for our weaving lesson," she said with a teasing smile. She knew that under normal conditions he would never have even considered learning a woman's craft.

Holding the toddler's hand, Willow headed back to the spot where she had found the mint. Once again she picked her pouch full, and then she began to cut the stems of the grass near the ground and stack it, until she had a bundle that was almost more than she could carry. She handed a few stems to Water Bug and coaxed him along until they dropped them near the shelter. She emptied the mint on a hide, where the rest dried. Back and forth they went collecting mint and grass, until Water Bug began to lag behind and whine. He was hot, tired and hungry.

Willow decided it was time for a break when she looked up and saw that the sun was well past the mid mark of the sky. Stripping Water Bugs clothes off, she sat him in the stream to cool and clean him. He giggled with delight and splashed, kicking his feet.

"Mother," he said. Had he really called her mother?

"Mother. Turdall?" He asked. He wanted her to find the turtle again. She searched the rocks in the vicinity, but couldn't find one.

"The turtle is gone. No turtle today." She said lifting him onto the grass so the sun and breeze could dry him. She carried him back to the shelter and dressed him. "Two Feathers has gone hunting. He will bring us a fine deer. We will have fresh meat to eat and more to dry for winter. I will make you a warm shirt and pants from the hide and my little Bug, one day soon, he will bring us a rabbit and I will be able to make you a pair of cozy moccasins before winter."

The boy lifted his arms to her, wanting to be held. She cuddled him and spooned in bites of soup she had made.

"Soon, you will be so heavy that I will not be able to pick you up, Water Bug. You have a good appetite and I know that one day you will be bigger and taller than Two Feathers."

Later, Willow continued to talk softly to him as she laid him on the blanket and used one corner to cover him. He was asleep. *I wonder if Two Feathers could make us some snares. I could make the baby warm clothes with the fur, before we leave. I know he will want to go as soon as the corn is dry.*

"Father, I am afraid. With winter coming and no adult to help us, how will we find a place that is good shelter against the cold? If we use the hides we have, to make a tent, it will be very small and won't have double walls to keep out the cold. It is getting cool at night. The season is changing. Help us Father, and help me to find the right words to tell Two Feathers about you."

She heard a whistle and call coming from the woods. She jumped up to look as Two Feathers came, leading his horse. Over its back rested a large deer. She clapped her hands to celebrate his success.

"Two Feathers, this is a very big deer. How did you get it so quickly? You have only been gone a few hours." She could see that he was proud of his success. As he pulled the deer to the grass, he was smiling.

"You are a good hunter." Under her breath, she thanked God for giving them more supplies for the hard months ahead.

"On the way back, I was thinking that I should set snares. We could dry more of the deer meat if we eat rabbit and you can use the pelts to make something for the boy."

"That is a good idea. He will need warmer clothes soon." She didn't say that she had been thinking the very same thing.

He ate some of the soup enjoying it.

"This is the best thing you have made so far. I was hungry on the way back and was wondering if you would have some food ready. Thank you, Willow. You work very hard."

"Thank you, Two Feathers; we will eat this winter because you are a good hunter. Come walk with me. Let's go check the corn. We can see Water Bug if he wakes." The field of corn held a plentiful crop. It had been planted as food for the entire village. Now there were only three people left to eat it. Each small cob held fat little kernels starting to dry and turn to seed.

"Soon we will be able to pick this and shell it. I guess I better have that weaving lesson when we get back. We should pick all of this and shell it out. We will need pouches to keep it in."

"I have only the smallest of skills, but I will show you what I know," she said humbly.

"Willow, as soon as the deer meat is dried and stored, I want to take a trip with you. I was in the woods alone for my three-night journey, when the raiders came. When I left here, I told my father that I would head north to the base of the mountains. He told me to be sure to find a shelter. He said it as if he knew of a cave there. I want to go with you and Bug to see if we can find it." She listened intently. "It will take us three days to reach the foothills. What do you think? It's worth a try isn't it?"

"Yes, it is and if we find a cave, it would leave us the hides we have to make winter clothes. I think it is a good idea."

"We should take all the horses with us. The exercise will be good for them. We couldn't leave them here hobbled, they are too vulnerable."

Willow was excited inside. "Father, I know that you have something ready for us that will get us safely through the winter. Thank you for answering my prayer so quickly."

When they returned to the shelter, Water Bug was starting to stir. Two Feathers picked him up and headed for the little stream. "Two, Two" said Water Bug happily, as he patted Two Feather's shoulder.

Willow had added wood to the camp fire and was preparing for their first session of weaving together, when Two Feathers sat down beside her and handed Water Bug his gourd toy.

"We should probably get the deer meat drying before we do weaving," she said. She pulled her father's knife from her pocket and realized that she should have saved his leather knife shield. It would protect my pocket from getting cut, she thought. Together they quickly worked to get the deer meat sliced and on the racks he had made.

He added a stingy little amount of wood to their fire, wishing that he didn't have to have a fire at all. He moved the racks as close as possible.

Later he watched as she struggled to get the first few rows of a large mat started. By the time the night grew dark he was well on his way to catching up with her and his work was smoother and tighter woven than hers.

CHAPTER FOUR
IT HAS TO BE TROUBLE

"It is hot this morning," Willow said, without looking up. She was splashing her face with the cool water of the stream.

"The meat will be dry and hard by tomorrow. It will feel good to leave this place and ride in the shade. This little stream grows wider as it gets nearer the mountains. There are flat rocks in the water to sit on. Water Bug will like that."

Now that it was decided, Willow was excited about going.

"I feel certain that Jesus will show us a shelter there. It will be good to be away from here with all its bad memories."

"Willow, you said Jesus is a God. How can you speak as if he will do your bidding?"

"He does not do my bidding, but He loves us and cares about us and I know that He doesn't want us to freeze this winter. He will show us a place. He has a plan for us and wants to show us His love, if we will let Him."

Two Feathers shook his head with doubt and walked over to one of the horses grazing near the shelter.

"I am going to ride each of the horses for a little exercise. They have been hobbled too long. I don't want them to grow weak. They need to move and run." He placed a soft bridle on the big black stallion and removed the hobble.

Instantly the horse began to prance and became difficult to handle. Two Feathers swung up on its bare

46

back and hung on with his knees and heels, as the horse tried to throw him. It bucked and bent low, trying to dislodge the weight on his back. Two Feathers hung on as the stallion spun around and tried to bite his leg. This was something that Two Feathers had been expecting. He jerked his leg up and the horse found its muzzle breathing into the leather-like sole of Two Feather's bare foot.

At once the muscles of the horse's legs pulled tight as he launched into a full speed run. The bucking was discontinued in hopes that he could leave his rider behind with speed. Two Feathers didn't try to rein him in. The flying hooves of the horse pounded a rhythm that matched Two Feather's excited heartbeat. Finally the horse slowed to a gallop and then Two Feathers eased him into a slower trot, and finally to a walk. The horse's beautiful black coat was lathered with sweat and he was tired. Two Feathers continued to walk him back to camp and around it until he had cooled.

Near the willow trees, he rubbed the horse down with grass dipped in the stream and then with dry grass until he was clean, cooled and dry. His coat shone. As he worked, he talked to him.

"You are a fine horse, big man. It has been too long since you were given a chance to show what you can do. I will ride you often. We will become good friends." Two Feathers tied the stallion near the stream where he had both sweet grass and water. "No more hobble for you. You are special."

Willow saw the respect and new bond between Two Feathers and the horse. She wasn't surprised. It was the finest horse she had ever seen, and they had

had many in the herd before the raiders came. She loved watching them.

"Two Feathers, I was thinking that I will put Water Bug on the tan mare, and ride one of the others myself, if you will pick one that is gentle enough for me. I could lead the mare and that way two would get a little exercise."

"You can ride my paint, if you want. She is gentle. You will enjoy her. I don't know the temperament of the others yet, so I cannot say that I would trust them. Your idea of riding one and leading another is good. I think I am going to get something to eat and then work with the two that you caught."

A few minutes later, Willow watched, as he slid up on the back of the brown mare with the black mane and tail. She seemed a little agitated but didn't buck. He cautiously took the rope from the tree branch that tethered the brown stallion and headed out of camp at a slow trot. Both horses seemed relieved to be loose and able to move freely. She watched until he was out of sight and then returned to her weaving. She knew that it was important to get as much done as possible.

When Two Feathers returned with the horses, he had a frown on his face. "What is wrong? Did something happen?"

"Nothing happened, they are both good horses." He had returned on the brown stallion. "I will rub him down, if you will do this one," he said, indicating the brown and black mare.

"Yes, of course," she said, coming quickly to the spot where he had stopped and dismounted. "You are still frowning. What is troubling you? I know it is not the horses. You love all of them. What is it?"

"I saw smoke from a camp fire as I rode. It is far away but I am sure it was a campfire. I do not like the idea of people so close to us. We do not need any more trouble."

"Why do you think it has to be? They might be able to help us."

"Willow, you think like a child! We need to put out our cooking fire and stay quiet until we are able to leave. I want to go check the corn again. Maybe we can pick it and take it with us. After I do that I will work with the rest of the horses, but I will be riding in the opposite direction."

Willow wondered if he had seen more than he was telling.

"Father, I am trusting in you. I will do what Two Feathers suggests, because I know that you are directing him." I hope the corn is ready for us to pick and shell she thought. I want to be gone from here before we are discovered.

"Willow, what are you thinking about? The horse is waiting to be rubbed down."

"I was just thinking about getting ready to leave. I have another mat nearly long enough to fold and stitch."

Two Feathers didn't reply, he seemed not to want to look directly at her and kept very busy rubbing the brown stallion.

As Willow rubbed the other horse she felt affection enter her heart for the mare. She scratched her ears and talked to her.

"You are a pretty lady and you gave him a good ride and didn't buck once. I think when you are used to us; you will be a very useful friend."

Just then, they heard a splash and a big wail. Willow had been distracted by caring for the horse and had forgotten to keep an eye on Water Bug. He had fallen into the stream. She scooped him up and checked to be sure he was not injured. She tried to quiet him, but he continued to cry.

"Can't you keep him quiet? I told you we need to be quiet," he yelled and stomped up to the campfire, pouring water on it and kicking dirt over it until it was out.

Willow knew that Two Feathers was worried and hiding something from her, but that didn't excuse the way he was acting. She was sure that he really wasn't angry with her. She carried the boy to the cornfield and checked several ears, to find they were dry and the kernels inside were hard. With Water Bug stripped and playing with a dandelion, she spread his clothes out in the sun to dry. She cut a piece of the roast and gave it to him to chew on, wondering how she would feed him with no fire to cook on.

Two Feathers had taken the rest of the horses for their run and was gone a long time. When he returned he seemed subdued.

"I am sorry that I yelled at you Willow, I guess I am just tired of trying to figure out a way for us to survive. I don't have all the answers, but I do know that we should get out of here as soon as we can, and take everything with us."

"Two Feathers, we will figure all this out together. You don't have to do it alone. I know that you don't believe in Jesus, yet. But I do and I know that He is helping us. And I have good news about the corn. It is ready to be picked."

"Can we put Water Bug on the mare for a while, where he will be safe?"

"I'll wrap his bottom and put him on one of the hides in his harness. His clothes will be dry by the time we finish for the night. It will be dark sooner for us, with no fire."

After Water Bug settled on the tan mare, Willow tied her in the shade beside the stream.

They each took a hide and headed for the corn field. Willow found that it was easier to leave the hide at the end of a row and bring her skirt full and dump it. When she looked over at Two Feathers she could see that he was hurrying to keep up with the pace she had set. By the time both hides were full and nearly too heavy to carry, it was growing dark.

Two Feathers rushed to camp and started a tiny fire. He felt bad that he had acted the way he had earlier and was trying hard to make up for it. Quickly gathering Water Bugs dry clothes, he dressed him and took him into the shelter. His mash was not warm, but the baby gladly accepted it. He was hungry. Willow dragged her load of corn up close to the fire and shelled a handful of kernels into a matate. With another smooth rock she crushed them, turning them to yellow powder. This was a chore she had done many times for her mother. She continued the process until she had scraped enough of the crushed corn into a pot, to make dough. She had gathered several cooking stones, in the village and this was the first time that she was going to try to use one. She smeared a layer of grease on the hot stone and waited for it to smoke, and then patted a small ball of the dough into a flat, thin cake and dropped it on the hot stone, pressing it still flatter.

When its edges were dry and starting to curl she flipped it over. "This doesn't look quite right, but we should be able to eat them," she said as she offered the first one to Two Feathers. He took it, tearing off a small piece and placing it in the fingers of the eager boy.

"He knows what that is and likes it. Look how he is stuffing his mouth," said Two Feathers with a chuckle. As Willow made more, they all had their fill and she learned the right time to turn them.

"The food was good Willow, Thank you."

"Let the fire die, we can shell the corn and gather the rest at first light. We should be able to leave before midday."

Two Feathers was pleased with the results of their efforts. Willow's weaving was looser and perfect to let air circulate around the dried meat. His was tighter and would hold the corn without the kernels escaping. Willow had even made time to make a small pouch, large enough to hold the dried mint. As he fastened the bundles on the horses, he had chosen the three they would ride. At first he thought, I will let the black stallion carry a load, he is strong. But he could destroy anything I put on his back if he starts bucking. I better ride him and put a bundle on my paint. Willow can ride the Black and brown mare and Water Bug can use the tan mare some of the time and ride in front of one of us the rest of the time. She is old and deserves the chance to travel some of the time, with no load.

"Willow, is there anything else that you want to take? You seem to have every cooking stone from the village. Do you really need to take so many? There are plenty of stones where we are going."

"These stones are special. They are seasoned from use and the food does not stick to them. If you have room, I want to take them all."

The hides had been used to bundle things onto the horses with ropes. The only thing left on the ground was the beautiful blanket Two Feather's mother had made.

"My mother made this blanket for me to take on my three day journey. I placed it on my pony. You should use it to ride on, so your legs don't get sore. I won't need it. My trousers are long enough to protect me from the horse's hair." He spread the blanket over the back of the brown and black mare and then saddled it for her. He helped her up. Water Bug was swinging his arms and making happy sounds as they headed into the woods. Two Feathers led the packhorses along the path he had taken before, beside the stream. Willow followed, leading the tan mare.

As soon as they were underway, Two Feathers started to relax. I will tell her what I saw, tonight when we camp. He knew they still were not safe. They were leaving a trail that a novice tracker could follow.

The patches of sun flickered through the trees, making the riders appreciate the breeze and the dense shade that covered them most of the time. Willow watched the water of the stream spill over rocks here and there creating tiny waterfalls and lovely refreshing tinkling sounds. She was enjoying the day, thinking that now they were underway, all would be fine and that they were safe.

It was late in the afternoon before they stopped to rest. As usual Water Bug wanted two things, to play in the water and to be fed. Willow did her best to take care of his needs and Two Feathers laughed, as the boy splashed the water so hard that it occasionally came up into his face.

"I think it is best if our trail is not left so obvious. I am going to take the horses and lead them across the stream and back to cross the trail a few times. If anyone tries to follow it will slow him down."

With no further explanation, he hopped on the paint and gathered the leads of all the horses.

"There is a clearing not far ahead, it will be a good place to camp tonight. The horses will have good grass there." She nodded agreement as he headed across the stream.

Water Bug was delighted when he saw the extra corn cakes she had baked at their last campfire. He held his hand out to get one and stuffed it in his mouth as soon as he had it in his grasp.

"You should still be getting milk," she said, "but water will have to do." She offered him sips from her cup and nibbled at a corn cake while she waited for Two Feathers to return. She was surprised when he rode up with the horses, out of the trees up stream. She offered him a corn cake, but he said he preferred to wait. After a few minutes Two Feathers lifted Water Bug up onto the horse into Willow's arms. She placed him facing forward and they headed out.

"We will ride in the water for a while. That way, there are no more tracks," he instructed. Very carefully he eased his horse and the ones he led into the stream. They would ride very slowly. He wanted to be sure that the horses didn't slip and get injured. Their footing wasn't as sure in the water.

Willow liked the slow pace. It didn't require much from her except to be sure that the sleeping boy didn't slip off. His head rested heavily on her left arm. It was beginning to ache. When he woke, she was grateful for the relief, but found his squirming hard to handle on the back of a horse. Two Feathers noticed as he checked behind him. He stopped the horses and made his way back to her.

"Let me take him," he said, scooping the active boy into his arms. Two Feathers returned to his horse, slid up with no problem and they were once again underway, without a print on the ground on either side of the stream.

When the clearing came into view, Willow was glad to stop for the night. She had never ridden that much in one day. Even at the slow pace, her muscles had become sore and her back stiff. As she slid down, she clamped her lips to keep from crying out. She wondered if she could walk. Cautiously, she moved away from her horse, trying not to show how she felt.

"Are you sore? You must be. I am, and I have ridden often."

"Yes, I am but I think if I walk around a little, it will be better." She didn't offer to take Water Bug, but instead, she stepped behind a bush at the edge of the stream and pulled her dress off. The cool water felt good on her skin. She washed and then quickly returned.

"Two Feathers, do you fish as well as you hunt? I saw sunfish in the stream while I was bathing."

"Fish would be a nice change for our meal. I will start a fire for you and then see if I can catch some."

Willow had cleaned Water Bug and led him, resisting all the way, to the center of the clearing, where she picked grain to add to the mash pot. The tall waving grass distracted him; he was easy to watch as she worked. She looked up at the trees, when she saw that his eyes were fixed in that direction. A beautiful doe watched them.

"Deer, Water Bug that was a deer," she said softly.

"Deer," he said, looking where it had been.

"Come, Water Bug, I will make some more corn cakes for tomorrow. They are good food to have when we travel. She looked through the packs until she found her favorite cooking stone. It had been her mothers. Placed near the fire, it would soon be hot enough to use. Proudly, Two Feathers brought four sunfish to the fire. He had cleaned them and speared them with a green branch.

"They are small, but they will taste good. Should I try to get more for tomorrow?"

"It wouldn't hurt to have a couple cooked and ready for Bug, when he gets hungry."

"I will try again, while these bake. They won't take very long."

He was having fun and forgot the time. It was nearly dark when he returned to the fire with four more fish.

"You are probably hungry. I was enjoying the fishing and lost track of the time. I hope you don't mind."

"Why would I mind? I knew where you were. We are safe and I must confess that I was enjoying myself, too. I fed Water Bug. He liked the fish, but it took a long time to get all the bones out. He ate two corn cakes and then fell asleep." She had wrapped him in the blanket and he looked comfortable and cozy.

"You take good care of him. He will grow up thinking of you as his mother."

"He is a good boy. He loves you, too. I am glad we have him. He is fun, and having him makes us more of a family."

As Two Feathers ate, he noticed that Willow was wrapping her arms around her bare legs and sitting closer to the fire. They had pulled the packs from the horses, so they could rest. The hides lay on top of the packs, where he had tossed them. He brought all of them, placing the stiffest one on the ground next to Water Bug. "Cover with this," he said, as he wrapped her in the softest one. I will use this one."

"Thank you, Two Feathers; I was getting a little chilled, and I am tired, but this has been a good day. I am going to lie beside Water Bug and watch the fire for a while."

The sounds of the forest were soft and comforting, as they rested. Silently, she prayed.

"Thank you, Jesus, for a good first day. It seems that we have traveled a long way, but the mountains still look far. Thank you, for watching over us, and for the food you gave us. I enjoyed the fish, and when we have other meat, we don't need to use our dried deer meat. Thank you, for Two Feathers and Water Bug. They are my family now. Teach me how to care for them. Give me the skills that I need to be a good mother for Water Bug. I love You, Jesus." She drifted off to a peaceful sleep.

CHAPTER FIVE
RIGHT IS NOT ALWAYS RIGHT

Two Feathers sat, wrapped in the hide near the fire, wondering what the coming days would bring. He wondered if he would be strong enough and wise enough to get them safely through the cold months ahead. There was movement on the other side of the fire. It caught his attention. Once again the lion sat across from him.

"Remember this, Two Feathers, right is not always right. Look down to be safe."

"What are you saying? I don't understand. What does that mean?"

"You will know when the time comes."

Two Feathers looked to his right but saw only darkness. And then he looked at the ground near his feet. He saw only dirt. When he looked up, the lion was gone.

Once again he checked for tracks, but there were none. He was left with a lasting impression of great power.

Suddenly he felt chilled. He added extra wood to the fire and curled up close to it. Willow and Water Bug slept on. He was sure that he had not been asleep and that the lion was not a dream.

They put the packs back on the horses and moved out as soon as they could. The day was hot and dry. Water Bug was back on the tan mare, and when Willow scratched her ears and hugged her, the horse seemed to be smiling.

"She seems to like being a babysitter," observed Willow as she swung up on the brown mare with the black mane and tail. "I want to give you a name, pretty lady. You are Lady. That will be your name. I think all the horses should have names. I think from now on the tan mare is going to be Grandmother. She takes good care of Bug."

"What did you say? I couldn't hear you," he asked.

"Nothing important, I was just talking to the horses." She smiled mischievously.

They were riding on the side of the stream again and moving along at a good pace. We make better time when we don't have to ride in the water, he thought. I wonder what Willow was mumbling about when we were leaving. I hope she isn't unhappy about something. Everything seems to be going along fairly well. She knows that I have been hiding our trail. I should probably stop putting it off and tell her what I saw, when I went riding, back at camp. When we stop I will tell her.

When Willow lowered the boy into the stream, she noticed that it felt warm, a lot warmer than it had been the day before. That is strange, since we are closer to the mountains, it should be cooler. Run off from a mountain is usually cold. Maybe this stream comes from somewhere beyond the mountains. She was puzzled. As she looked around, she noticed many plants that she had never seen before. Huge woody Vines wrapped around some of the trees and disappeared through the canopy of leaves above her. Some of the trees were different, too. I wish I knew which plants could be eaten. I am hungry for greens.

Willow sat quietly beside Water Bug, as he played in the water. She cupped her hand to take a drink. The water tastes strange. There is something different here. She suddenly felt uncertain about his safety, and pulled Water Bug from the water. He protested, but she insisted, hastily pulling his clothes back on.

"Have you noticed anything different here?" Two Feathers asked as he walked near with a frown on his face. "It feels damp here, almost steamy. I don't know how that is possible when it hasn't rained in a week or more.

"Two Feathers, have you touched the water?"

"No. Why?"

"Touch it. It feels warmer than yesterday. How is that possible? It tastes different, too."

Two Feathers, knelt by the water and cupped a bit to his lips, but didn't drink it. "It does smell odd. Did the boy drink any?"

"No, and I took him out of the water as soon as I realized that something was strange. Let's move on. I don't like it here."

In spite of the lush greenery, they didn't like what they couldn't understand or explain.

"The horses all drank. I hope it doesn't make them sick," he said, as he swung up on the black stallion.

Willow had put Water Bug back on Grandmother, with a piece of meat in one hand and a corn cake in the other. She had offered him a drink from the pot of water she had brought from the campsite. They were all fine for now.

An hour later, Two Feathers slid from the stallion and came back to talk to her. "The stream splits ahead. I want to check the water in both branches. She tied

Lady and Grandmother to a tree near the stream, and bent to touch the water. It was very warm.

The horses backed away.

"I am coming with you. I hope that we find good water soon. The horses need it and so do we."

"Look over there. The stream is actually steaming." That was when they noticed that their feet were getting warm. "The rocks are heated from beneath. The mountain has a fire inside. Look over there. The rocks are split and you can see down inside to a red glow deep inside. That must be the fire."

"Willow was frightened. "This is not a safe place. Let's go back. I don't like it here."

When they approached the spot where the two streams joined, they could tell that the left stream was cool and clear. "Do you want to go up this way on foot? He asked.

"No, I think we can get back on the horses and follow the left side. I don't think that right is right."

Her statement of the obvious hit him like a bolt of lightning.

That is what the Lion Spirit told me. He was amazed.

"If we had ridden the horses that direction, there is no way to know what could have happened. They might have broken through the stone crust, or stepped into the water and burned their feet! I must think what else he said. It is hard to remember. It didn't make sense at the time."

"Now I remember," he said, "Look down to be safe." I better lead with caution. Now, he was certain that the lion was helping them.

He led so slowly that it was aggravating Willow. She could not hear what he was saying. She didn't know that Two Feathers was examining every step that the stallion took.

When he stopped, she could not see a reason for it. It was too soon to stop and rest. She was eager to locate a cave.

"Why are we stopping?" She called out in frustration.

"Tie the horses and come here." Lady and Grandmother eagerly took a long drink from the stream.

"Sit beside me on this rock. Willow we need to talk. Last night after you went to sleep, I saw the Spirit Lion again. It said right is not always right. Look down to be safe."

"You saw a lion at our camp? You must have been dreaming."

"I saw him before remember? He told me to return to camp, that I was needed. That's when I came back with the deer and found you and Water Bug after the raid. He is very real. He speaks and what he has said each time has been true. Last night, he also said, "Look down to be safe. Now look ahead of us on the ground where we might have ridden.""

"Oh, Two Feathers, It looks like a giant crack in the earth. I am so glad that you stopped us."

"The Spirit Lion didn't say; look down so you don't fall. He said, look down to be safe. I think we need to go investigate that crack. Water Bug is fine for a few more minutes."

Willow walked hesitantly toward, what looked like a huge fissure in the ground. As they stood near the edge, they followed it with their eyes in both directions.

"It seems to continue into the mountain. The other way, it disappears into the trees," she couldn't see how this could be of help to them.

"Do you want to see where it starts?"

"Yes, but I will take my patches. I think you should check on Bug, and give him a drink. Don't let him get in the water, I may be right back."

She lifted the heavy boy down and he immediately headed for the water.

"No, Water Bug let me give you a drink and a corn cake instead. She led him to a spot of green grass between the trees and sat him down, handing him a cup. With both hands, he managed his own drink.

"You were thirsty. Weren't you?" She poured a little more water in the cup and offered it to him.

"Drink," he said as he took it again. "Drink," he said with delight as he poured the water onto the grass.

She handed him a small piece of corn cake, hoping that by holding on to the rest of it in front of him, that it would hold his interest a little longer. He reached for the rest of it and she relented, letting him take it. As usual, he stuffed as much of it as he could into his mouth. With his cheeks billowing out like those of a greedy squirrel, he once again headed for the stream as fast as his legs could carry him.

Willow picked him up and turned as she saw Two Feathers returning. He had a wide smile on his face as he reached down to take the boy.

"Get on your horse and follow me." She felt a flutter of excitement as she got up on Lady and led

Grandmother. Two Feathers was leading the packhorses along ahead of her through the trees.

When he stopped, he said, I think that we should take the horses in with us at least a little way. That way they are out of sight. This crack or cave goes back into the mountain a long way." Willow was beginning to wonder if this was the cave they were looking for. The horse's hooves made a loud echoing sound as they walked on the rock base. The walls seemed smooth and the rocks resembled folds in dough. She was noticing the soft shades of color, in the cave walls, when Two Feathers stopped and stepped down. "We can walk in a little farther, but it gets darker as you go."

"Were you in here, already?"

"Yes, when I saw what it was, I couldn't resist. Willow, I think we could make this cave a comfortable place to spend the winter."

"It is very big, Two Feathers. Do you think we could keep it warm enough?"

"It is warmer in here, than outside. I think the fire in the mountain heats it a little, and with the entrance down the way it is, the wind doesn't come in."

"Two Feathers, I am not sure. I like it and I think it could work, but I want to stay in the woods for tonight. We need to pray about it and watch the entrance to see if any animals are using this cave."

Two Feathers was disappointed. He wanted to move right in, but he thought she was probably right to be wary.

"Willow when we rode here, did you notice that the stream disappears into the mountain? I wonder where it goes, I mean where it comes from. It has to start here somewhere."

"No, I guess I didn't. I am just glad that it isn't hot and smelly like the other side. The horses are glad, too."

Two feathers cleared a wide circle on the ground near the tall pines and built a small fire in the center.

As they removed the packs from the horses, Willow was thinking that tonight she would ask again, what he had seen back at camp that had caused him to want to leave right away.

"Willow, I need to tell you something. When I was riding the stallion that day, I saw the raider's camp, but I didn't tell you. I crept up close to be sure. They had our Chief there. He was tied, hanging in the branches of a tree. He was dead. I feel that if they decided to return to the village, they would know that someone of the people was still alive. They would track us, and kill us, too. That is why I tried to hide our trail. I wasn't completely open with you, but it was because I didn't want you to be frightened."

Willow's eyes grew large as she listened.

"Thank you, Two Feathers. I knew there was something more to it. I could sense it. Do you know the people the raiders came from?"

"No, but I think that either of us would recognize them.

"As we travel, we will need to be watchful."

"Yes, but right now we need to be observant to see if there are animals in that cave. I think we should scatter dirt in the mouth of it. If anything goes in or out while we sleep we will see the prints. Stepping on the rocks doesn't leave a trail."

"That is a good idea, Willow. I'll do it right now."

They camped outside for two days, until they felt sure that no animal was claiming the cave as home. When they entered the cave, Water Bug soon learned that the cave echoed. He would yell and screech, to listen to the sound.

"I will be glad when he tires of that," said Willow, as she arranged the hides to make a sleeping area. Suddenly Water Bug was quiet.

When she turned around, she couldn't see him. He was gone!

Willow yelled his name and ran outside to tell Two Feathers and raced back in, shouting.

"Water Bug, where are you?" Tears streamed down her face. "Two Feathers, he might have wandered into the dark. We could lose him forever. We have to find him now!" She was frantic.

Two Feathers was equally concerned, he had seen cracks in the floor big enough to fall into. There was no way to know how deep they were.

"Quiet. Willow. Be quiet. Listen." They could hear his happy, chirpy sounds, but as the sounds bounced off the rock walls here and there, it was impossible to tell where they were coming from. "Stay here and stand still, I will be right back." Two Feathers ran to the campfire lighting two long dry branches and returned with them. "Here, we need these for light and to mark our path. You go down that side of the wall. I will walk close to this one. Use the tip of the branch to leave a black smudge now and then so you can follow them back and watch where you step." It was only a moment before Two Feathers was calling Willow's name with excitement. "Willow, he is here. Come see what our boy has found."

66

"Oh, Water Bug," she said, dropping the burning branch and picking him up to hold him close. It was then that she noticed that he was soaking wet.

"He found a separate room with water! He must have followed the sound. It sounds like the stream in here, but there is only this little trickle on the wall and the puddle on the floor, before it disappears into that little hole." Two Feathers was happy over finding the boy and the convenient water supply.

"This is wonderful," said Willow. We can have drinking water and water to cook and wash, without going out to the stream." Two Feathers cupped his hand and let the water fill his palm. He sipped it and smiled. It is cold and delicious."

He looked up at the ceiling and walls of the room. "There is an opening there on the side that is letting in a little bit of light. During the day we can come in here to get water without a torch. Willow, do you see what I do? This whole room sparkles!"

"The heat in the mountain has made crystals. It is so beautiful!" They stood in awe.

"Two Feathers catch him. He is exploring again."

"Come here my soggy Bug," he said, as he swung the toddler onto his shoulders.

Let's go see what he was interested in."

As they stepped through the opening and followed around a huge fold in the formation of rock, they found themselves walking on soft blue-green grass, under ancient twisted trees.

"This is strange. It seems to have no way out except through the cave. This is like a Garden of Eden, inside the mountain," said Willow.

"What is a Garden of Eden?"

"It is a beautiful garden, that God made for the first man and woman, but they sinned by breaking his rule and he put them out of the garden. It is in the real creation story."

"This looks like a safe place for Water Bug to play. This garden is big and walled in on all sides. It is a perfect place to bring the horses." As they walked a little further, they could hear water once again.

"Look, Two Feathers, the water seeps out of the rocks up there and falls to this perfect basin, from there it runs along and goes under those rocks. The horses will have water without us carrying it. We could not have planned a better place."

Two Feathers was climbing the rocks near the waterfall before she finished speaking. "Willow, I will come down and hold onto Water Bug. You will want to see this."

It was harder for Willow to pull herself up, but it was worth the effort. Spread before her, as far as she could see, was water, sparkling blue, fresh water.

"Two Feathers, I have never seen so much water. It is beautiful."

"I think we have found the source of water for the stream," said Two Feathers.

"This is so exciting," she said. "It is like a different world here. I cannot believe all this is real. I wonder if we are the first people to ever see this garden."

"I don't know Willow, but it is late, we need to feed Bug, and then bring the horses in here. It is a good place."

"I knew that God would give us a safe, warm, winter lodge. Thank you, Jesus. You never disappoint me. This is so much more than I could ever imagine."

"Two Feathers, will you start us a small fire in here, while I get Bug comfortable?"

"Yes, but while I am busy, be careful. Watch the boy every minute. I am glad that he didn't go any farther. We should learn a lesson from that. I need to block off the back part of the cave to make it safe for him. There are some big cracks back there in the dark that I noticed earlier. We have to keep him with us at all times until we can make it safe."

"Yes, you are right. Thank you, Two Feathers." Willow carried a pot in one hand and led Water Bug to the water, with the other. Two Feathers feels that we have discovered the perfect place. It seems almost too perfect. Then wWhy do I have an uneasy feeling, she asked herself as she filled the pot? I don't see anything that I would change but it all just seems a little creepy.

"Would you like to take your clothes off and play in the water for a little while? She asked as she pulled his shirt over his head. He lifted his face and giggled as the small stream of water splashed on his face. He stomped and plopped his bare bottom in the puddle laughing. "If anyone could see you, they would know why we call you Water Bug. You are always happy when you can play in water. Look at that round tummy and chubby legs. You are certainly not going hungry.

Loving water saved your life, little one. If you hadn't been in the water that day, you wouldn't be here now." She knew that she was allowing herself to remember again. That horrible day slammed into her thoughts often.

"No, I don't want to be sad today," she said, closing the door in her mind and shutting the horror out. "This is a marvelous, joyous day. We have a home that is safe and warm, and very special."

Two Feathers brought in Lady and Grandmother first, walking them slowly past the little cooking fire he had started and through the opening in the wall out into the beautiful garden.

"You will not need these," he said, as he removed their bridles and lead ropes. "It is good that they can be free, with nature providing all the food and water they need."

Willow was thinking it was very peculiar that no animals were in the cave or birds in the garden trees. She had been watching for any sign, but didn't see any.

"This is the last horse," he said, as he rode the paint slowly past. "I am going back outside before it gets totally dark and brush away any prints. I will be back in a few minutes. He decided to walk beyond the cave to see if he could see any part of the lake. He couldn't. I think if I climb up the side of the mountain, I could probably find a way in and come back through the garden. I haven't enough daylight left. I'll try that some other time. It is nearly dark.

Two Feathers made sure that the fire they had used outside was totally out and he had put leaves over the bare circle and dropped branches here and there, to make it look natural. There was nothing left, to cause detection.

Willow had placed their pouches and packs across the floor so that she had to step over them to get to the room with the water. It wouldn't stop Water Bug if he was determined to go, but it would slow him down. He would have to crawl over. Two Feathers smiled his approval when he entered.

"Tomorrow, I will make a gate for the opening to the garden, and I will bring in branches to block this part off from the rest. It will be fun to investigate back further, but first we need to make this part secure for him."

Sleep came easily to Two Feathers. For the first time since the raid he felt protected and safe. Willow couldn't sleep. She was concerned that Water Bug might wake up before they did, and get in trouble. She solved the problem, by tying a long cord to his ankle and then around her wrist. He could toss and roll over but not move away undetected. After that she was able to sleep.

During the night she heard strange gurgles and rumbles with small vibrations, but it was not enough to be alarming. That is probably why there are no animals here, she thought. They don't understand the activity in the mountain and it frightens them away. I hope the horses will be able to adjust.

The next morning Willow noticed that Two Feathers seemed nervous as he moved about checking their food supply and the horses.

"What are you thinking about, Two Feathers? You have checked the dried meat and corn more than once. I am sure that it is fine."

"Willow I need to go back to the village and beyond, where the raiders had our Chief. I was trying to make myself comfortable with the thought that you would be all right here, alone for a few days. I can't leave our Chief there and not send his spirit on to the next world. I must pray for the Chief as we did for all our people. You will be safe here and there is plenty of food."

"The boy and I will be fine here, but I am not sure that you will be. What will you do if the raiders are still in the area? If they spot you, they will kill you."

"Yes, I know. It will be necessary to use caution, but they are probably gone by now. There is nothing there to hold their interest. I plan to circle around so that my tracks will not lead anyone back here. I have been thinking about this all the time we were traveling. Don't worry Willow. You and the boy are my family now. I will come back to you as soon as I can."

CHAPTER SIX
BE BRAVE LITTLE SISTER

"The sun is up and the day is warm. Take food and go. You will be able to travel easily alone. We will look for your return."

Two Feathers chose the mare that Willow liked.

"She will blend with the trees and if I need to leave her tied, she will be difficult for anyone to spot." He picked up Water Bug and held him close for a moment.

"Be a good boy while I am gone," he said.

"Two. Two," The boy said coaxing to be lifted again as Two Feathers turned to Willow.

"Be brave, little sister. I will return soon."

"I will pray for you," she said as he turned the horse in the direction they had come. "Be safe, my brother. Don't worry about us. We will build that wall of branches while you are gone." Softly she said, "Please guard him Father."

"Come, Bug, we have lots of work to do." She handed him a small twig and gathered several branches in her arms before heading slowly back into the cave, while watching Water Bug toddle along near her. He stopped to pick up a shiny stone, leaving the twig behind.

The barricade took many trips outside to complete a small section. Soon Willow realized just how tired she was. After a little lunch, she curled up near the fire cuddling the sleepy boy. He had started sucking his thumb before he had finished eating.

"Even though you will probably sleep longer than I do, I am not taking any chances," she said as she fastened the cord to his ankle. "If anything ever

73

happened to you, I would never forgive myself. I am your mother now and I love you." She kissed the top of his head and pushed his moist hair from his forehead.

When Willow woke up, she felt hot and sticky. Water Bug's hair was plastered to his neck with sweat and his cheeks were pink. Why is it so hot? She wondered. Untying the cord from his ankle she wrapped it around her waist and tied it. She lifted the heavy baby and walked outside. It was cloudy and the soft breeze felt refreshing. The mountain must be sending heat into this area, under the cave. I hope it is safe. She made her way back inside and over the barricade where she stopped by the water, allowing it to run across the palms of her hands, splashing her face and neck. Water Bug eagerly played in the water, squatting down and sipping it from the puddle and enjoying the cold trickle as it ran down his body.

"Let's go see what the horses are doing," she said as she led him out into the sunshine of the garden.

Suddenly a strong rumble sent vibrations under her feet causing her to nearly loose her balance.

"I don't think this mountain is sleeping! Father, God, I feel that this is not a safe place for us to stay. I need to take the horses out of here," she said hurrying away from the rocks of the opening. Where are the horses? She thought. I can't see them. She was nearly running, with the boy in her arms, when she saw them, bunched together at the far end of the small meadow. The poor things are afraid. So am I. If the cave collapses there isn't a way to take them out of here.

I think I better move them out under the trees by the entrance of the cave until we know this mountain better. Willow slid up on Grandmother after tying the cord from her waist, around the neck of the paint. With only her knees she directed the gentle old mare and led the paint out to the trees. Grandmother, I must quickly put Water Bug on your back for safekeeping. The other horses need to be brought out."

With the harness she had quickly grabbed on the way out, she fastened the boy where she felt he would be safe. A sense of urgency sent pangs of alarm into her chest.

She ran through the cave, collecting the coiled ropes on the way. All the horses were easy to handle, except the black stallion. Now he was agitated and sensed her nervousness. He pranced away each time she got near.

"Do you want to stay here all alone? Fine!" She said in frustration and fear, stomping her foot. She gathered the leads in her hands and headed for the entrance. Another rumble and vibration beneath her feet caused her to run. The black stallion broke through the ancient trees and darted past her going to the entrance. She could hear his hooves on the rock of the cave floor as he dashed toward the light at the opening.

"Good. That gets him out where he is safe. I will worry about catching him when he calms down," she said

"It is going to be alright. Come on, now, that's it. Through here and we are almost out." She tried to reassure the horses as she hurried them along. Another rumble dropped several rocks into the cave and the horses panicked, bolting past her, jerking the ropes from her hands. At least they are clear, she thought.

"Father, please help me to save the bags of food," she cried out in terror, dragging out the bags of corn, next the bags of meat and another bag of corn.

"I have to get everything out of here right now! If it collapses I won't be able to get to them."

She was racing in and dragging things out as fast as she could, when the strongest tremor yet, sent her tumbling to the floor of the cave. She crawled with the blanket gathering several pots and cooking utensils forming a bundle. The mountain continued to make strange sounds and then all at once she heard a tinkling sound as the ceiling of the water room began to drop its crystals. A fierce shake sent several pieces bouncing into the cave at her feet. Willow grabbed one stuffing it into her pocket and before lifting the heavy blanket, swiftly stepping over fallen rocks, she rushed to the entrance.

It was then that she realized that all the horses had gone farther than she had intended. None were visible in the immediate area. I need to go in the cave one last time to bring out the hides and my mother's cooking stone.

"Father, I am terrified. Be with me and help me to do this, and please watch over Water Bug."

Bravely, she reentered the cave, making her way to their campsite. As she gathered the hides and heavy stones in her arms, she realized that the soles of her feet were so hot that they were hurting more with each step.

"This floor is getting hotter! I have to get out of here!" A hole in the wall beside her began to whistle, releasing steam.

As she turned to the entrance a crack opened in the floor and began to widen, exposing the red-hot lava running beneath it. She screamed and leapt the fissure, as it grew still wider. Without looking back she ran to the opening of the cave, not allowing herself to think or doubt that she would make it. As she cleared the opening, standing in the sunshine, she stopped to catch her breath, only to be engulfed by a cloud of dust and smoke rolling from the cave causing her to cough and choke as her lungs objected to the toxic ash in the air.

"Thank You Father, for helping me out of there just in time," she said. After a few minutes of sitting under the trees trying to clear her lungs she began to search for Water Bug and the horses.

"Where are the horses? Where is my Water Bug? Water Bug, where are you? Water Bug," she called. What if Grandmother has taken him a long ways? I may not find them, she thought, feeling frightened at the possibility. She studied the ground hoping to find prints that would lead her to the mare with the boy on its back. She listened, standing totally still, not breathing. She heard something, a small sound, from deeper in the woods. She couldn't tell if she had heard a bird or a sound made by the boy. I have to find him soon. It will be dark before long. I should have taken the time to tie the old mare carefully. I was hurrying to get the horses out and now I can't find them!

"Oh God, help me to find Water Bug!"

As she circled a large clump of bushes, there in front of her grazing peacefully, were the horses, including Grandmother.

"Thank you Father, Oh Thank you," she said as she approached the horses. Sliding up behind Water Bug, she guided the old mare close enough to the others that she was able to reach their leads. I doubt if I will find the black tonight, but my Bug is safe. She kissed his cheek as he whined a little rubbing his eyes.

"Yes, I know that you are hungry and tired. We will make a camp back by the stream, away from the mountain, back where the water is cool." She stopped near the cave just long enough to tie all the bundles on the other horses.

"Let's go my little Bug. You will be glad to be down and fed soon." She directed the horses back along the cool side of the stream beyond where the two joined and rode until nearly dark. Finally, when she put her hand in the water it was cool.

She chose a place in the trees and pulled the packs off the horses.

"You have served me well today, my friends. I will tie you near the stream where you can eat the sweet grass and drink," she said. Water Bug was fussing loudly. He wanted to play in the water and to be fed. He was tired of being on the mare's back. Willow lifted him down and held him close for a moment, thinking how good God was to protect them and give them a warning so they could get out of the cave unharmed.

"Thank you again, Father. Be with us always. I must learn to listen more closely to your guidance. I thought that cave was where you wanted us. There must be another place for us somewhere that is safe. I know that you will give us shelter for the coming winter."

Later, as she looked at the sleeping boy wrapped in the blanket, she grasped that God had spared them again.

"Father, you shielded us from the raiders and now protected us from the mountain of fire. I can't help wondering why."

She had cleared a small area and had finally managed to get a fire going. Her mother's cooking stone sat near the fire, shining from the grease of many years of use. I am glad that I saved it. When I look at it, I feel like somehow my mother is close to me. The small pot containing grease sat nearby, and a large cooking pot containing water and dried meat simmered in the heat. In the morning I will make corn cakes. They are his favorite food.

In her hand, she held the crystal from the cave. This is beautiful. I hope that Two Feathers can drill a hole in it. I would like to make a necklace.

Gently she placed the cord around Water Bugs ankle and then secured it around her wrist. As she curled up near him, she knew that sleep would not come easily this night. She was alone in the dark and missed the security of Two Feather's presence. She could still hear the rumbles of the mountain.

As she lay there quietly; her hand sought the sole of her foot. It hurt. Both feet hurt. She had been too busy earlier to concern herself with it, but now in the dark she felt the blisters. I need to wash my feet and coat them with grease. I must have burned them in the cave. Now that she had acknowledged the discomfort, it seemed to grow. Releasing the cord from her wrist, she limped to the stream a short distance away. Each step was painful. She sat on a rock and placed her feet in the stream. This is pleasant, she thought. Without thinking about it, she slipped her clothes off and lowered herself into the water. It felt good to wash the ash and dust from her hair and body and she enjoyed the fresh feeling of the water in the darkness.

Back by the fire she coated her soles with grease and tied the cord to her wrist. Covering herself completely with the hide, she finally slept in her little cocoon.

A tug and another on her wrist woke her in the morning. Water Bug was trying to get to the stream. He was happy, hungry and ready to play. After a bath, she settled him on the grass with a cup of water and a piece of soft meat from the pot, while she made the corn cakes. As soon as it was cool enough she gave him the first one and he stuffed half of it in his mouth. Willow made a large stack and placed them in a pot, covering the top. As soon as you are finished eating we need to go search for the black horse.

He began to whine as she settled him into his harness on the mare.

"Don't worry, my Bug, today I will be riding with you." After making sure that the fire was safe to leave, she headed back along the stream, the way they had come the night before. Just as she suspected, as the day grew warm, the horse had moved to the stream to get a drink. She was not able to get a lead on him. He stood a few yards off, and blew a greeting but moved away when she approached with a rope. I wish I had Two Feathers talent with horses. He will have to catch that one, she thought, as she returned to her camp.

When she looked in the direction of the mountains, she saw flames at the top of the trees in the distance and a wall of smoke in the sky.

"Oh Father, the mountain has set the trees on fire. I have got to move away as fast as I can!"

80

With all the packs and sacks quickly fastened on the horses, she placed a bridle on the paint and headed in the direction of the village. This way I will be able to meet Two Feathers somewhere along the way, she thought, as they moved out. When she heard pounding hooves move up and pass by, she saw that the stallion was leading the way. As long as he follows the path of the stream, I will follow him, she thought, hurrying the paint to match the swift pace the black stallion was setting.

When she looked back she could see that the fire was closer.

"It is gaining on us. I don't know if we can outrun it!

It didn't take long before the old mare with Water Bug on her back, grew tired and couldn't keep up the pace.

"Poor Grandmother, I will take the boy, but removing his weight won't give you much relief. He isn't very heavy. We have to keep moving." Willow slid the boy in front of her on the paint.

"Father, we are in grave danger. The fire is getting closer and the horses are tiring. Help us. I don't know what to do!"

Suddenly, a breeze blew in Willow's face, giving her a breath of fresh air, free of smoke.

"If the wind pushes the flames back toward the mountain, we will be able to escape. Thank you, Father." They hurried on for another half hour, and finally she felt that she could stop to let the horses drink and rest.

"This is a hot day, for late fall," she said to Bug as she watched him splash in the shallow stream. She placed her feet in the cool water and looked in the

81

direction of the fire. She could see billows of smoke in the sky, but the fire was farther away. The breeze continued to blow north the rest of the day.

"Thank you, Jesus for watching over us. Give me wisdom to keep us safe, and please keep Two Feathers from harm and bring him back to us, soon."

With soft cooked meat, wrapped in a corn cake, they moved on with Willow stuffing bites into Water Bugs mouth. When she handed him a cup with water, he deliberately poured it out onto the horse's neck, laughing as it ran down.

"Water Bug, you were supposed to drink that not pour it on the horse. You will be thirsty soon." The boy always drank from the stream when he was playing, so for now, he was fine. Soon his thumb made its way into his mouth, and he slept with his head resting against her.

As the shadows grew long, Willow realized that they were near the clearing where they had camped before. She led the horses through the trees and tied them on the edge of the open grass. The camp gave her a feeling of comfort as she lit a small fire in the bare circle they had made just days before. In the distance, she heard thunder. The horizon wasn't visible because of the trees, but the wind had shifted a little and carried a chilly dampness, that spoke of rain.

Quickly Willow hacked at leafy branches to repair the shelter they had used. Dead branches under the pine boughs were not very strong, but she snapped them off and tied them upright, placing stones at their bases. Two more branches across the top to form a roof and then the stiff hide, with the leafy branches tied on top. She hoped that the trees above would offer some coverage too. With their corn and dried meat dragged inside, she put a hide on top of them punching and pushing to make the surface as smooth as possible to sit on.

The wind grew stronger, and soon she brought the horses beside the shelter. It would act as a windbreak for them. Their small fire had to be put out. Sparks were flying in the wind. I don't want to deal with another fire, not for a long time, she thought, not ever.

As they cuddled together under the blanket, the little shelter shifted back and forth in the wind.

"I hope this holds together, or we and the food will be very wet." In spite of the scraping branches and the wind rustling the trees, Willow slept. It didn't rain. The ground was dry when she woke.

Beside the shelter, the horses were restless. "I will move you to the water, my friends," she said as she led them and secured each to a spot along the stream. "I think we will stay right here, until Two Feathers returns. He will see that we are here."

The day passed quietly and Willow sat weaving a mat, allowing her feet to heal. Water Bug wandered around in the tall grass of the clearing, plopping down occasionally to inspect something, but never far. The next day was like the previous. Their third day began with a roll of thunder that brought the rain that it promised. Willow had made the effort to strengthen the shelter and was glad when she sat inside it entertaining Water Bug with a cup, allowing him to catch the drips as they fell from the roof.

"Rain, rain," he said.

"Yes, rain. You are a smart boy. We haven't seen rain in quite a while. I am pleased that you remember the word."

"Two. Two," he said with a big grin as Two Feathers bent low and crawled in beside them taking the boy on his lap.

"I am glad that you are back with us. We missed you. These are not easy times. Did you find our Chief? Were the raiders gone?"

"I am glad to be back with you, too. The raiders were gone. All I did was pile dry brush against the singular pine tree he was in and set it on fire. I stayed there until it had burned completely and then buried his bones. But, why are you here and not in the cave? I knew exactly where to find you when I saw the horses tied along the stream."

"Oh, Two Feathers, it was as terrifying as the raid on the village! The mountain is not sleeping! It began to shake and rumble and several times I lost my balance trying to get the horses out of the garden before the cave might collapse. Rocks were falling and the floor split and there was fire under it and steam. Then when I finally got everything out, the horses had gone into the woods farther than I thought they would and I had to find them because Water Bug was on Grandmother. I caught all the horses but the black stallion. He is near though, because when the mountain set the trees on fire, he led us back this way along the stream. The fire was gaining on us until I prayed and God changed the direction of the wind and pushed the fire back toward the mountain."

"You really have had a terrible time. I am sorry that I wasn't here to help you. It is my fault. I should have known that the cave wouldn't be safe. We saw the fire in that mountain on the other side. What was I thinking?"

"Don't blame yourself Two Feathers; I wanted it to be our winter lodge so that we would know that we were safe for winter and not have to search anymore. Neither of us used good judgment."

"I am glad that you got out when you did. You could have both been killed! You even saved the horses. They must have been hard to handle with the ground shaking and rocks falling."

"It wasn't too hard to get lead ropes on them, but they got more frightened in the cave when rocks were falling and dashed past me and out into the woods. I couldn't get a rope on the black stallion. He ran out ahead of us. He is pretty smart."

"Tomorrow, I will search until I find him." Water Bug reached up and patted his face and screeched.

"I think he wants my attention. How are you boy? Were you afraid?" He tickled the boy and blew in his neck, making a sound.

"I wonder if he knew that he was in danger. This little guy has been through a lot. We all have been."

"Two Feathers, are you hungry? I made some corn cakes and have grain cooked and meat softened."

"Thank you Willow, I would like something." As Willow got up to get his food he noticed that she was limping.

"What happened to your feet?"

"The floor of the cave was very hot by the time I got everything out. I burned them. They are healing now. In a few days they will be fine."

"I am so sorry, Willow, Please sit back down with Water Bug. I will get some food for all of us."

"Thank you, Two Feathers; I hope the rain is not in our food. I put pots over the tops to cover it."

"Everything is fine." He handed Water Bug a corn cake and a piece of the soft meat. "Your corn cakes are getting better. The men in this family appreciate your cooking, Willow," he said laughing. Water Bug stuffed his mouth as usual and tried to crawl out into the rain. "No you don't, little man. Stay here," he said, plopping the boy down between them.

"Two Feathers we need to make a decision on where we will look for a winter shelter and head out soon. Winter will be here sooner than we would like."

"Yes, we need to leave as soon as I catch the stallion. I keep thinking about what the Lion said. Maybe we need to go back to the mountain and beyond it. We know now that there is a large lake there, and the garden had wonderful trees in it. That means that the ground in that area is good for growing. Maybe we can find a shelter somewhere on the other side of the water. What do you think?"

"Do you really want to go back there? That fire is probably still burning. We will have to go around it."

"Maybe this rain will put the fire out. Don't worry little sister. If I have to, I will build us a shelter, like this, only bigger and thicker. You built this while caring for a baby and with burned feet. I guess we could work as a team and build a really good winter shelter, if we have to."

"That is a good idea. All of a sudden I am eager to get going. If this rain stops maybe you can find the stallion tonight, and we can head out in the morning."

CHAPTER SEVEN
WILLOW IS SPENT

Two Feathers began his search for the black stallion as soon as the rain let up. He found him soon after, not far from the other horses on the other side of the stream. It took him a little while to coax the big horse to come to him, but once the rope was on his neck he walked along calmly. Two Feathers slipped a bridle on him and swung up, dropping the lead rope to the grass.

"I will be back before dark," he said as he rode away in the direction of the fire. He circled left to see how far the fire had reached. Talking to the horse, scratching and praising him, he stopped when the darkened trees gave way to green again.

The fire must have been terrifying. I am so glad that they were not caught in it, he thought, allowing the scene to convey its frightening dimensions and power to his very soul.

After tying the favored horse near the stream, Two Feathers joined Willow at their small campfire.

"I followed the fire-line to its edge, and if we want to, we can circle it to the left and not ride through the burned area."

"Good. It will be more pleasant if we don't have to ride through charred trees and ashes and Water Bug will ride better and not whine to get down if he can't see the stream. I wonder what he will think when he sees the lake. I will have to watch him when we are near it. He will want to charge right in."

"Well we can worry about that when the time comes. For now we should all get some sleep."

The shelter wasn't large enough for all of them to sleep comfortably. Two Feathers slept near the fire but several times during the night, he heard Willow cry out as the terror of the alarming events haunted her sleep.

As they packed things up and loaded them onto the horses, Two Feathers noticed how tired Willow looked. She doesn't sleep well and isn't eating much either. I hope that we can find a place soon so she can begin to rest and heal inside. I know that her heart still hurts. She yearns for her family just as I long for mine. She was so brave, dealing with the mountain. I don't know if I would have kept going back in like she did. He felt a great deal of respect for the strong, courageous will that she had shown.

Riding the black stallion, Two Feathers led the way. The day was warm and sunny. Riding in the shade of the trees was just cool enough to be comfortable. They moved at a steady pace and rode outside of the fire-line, most of the day. When they stopped, Two Feathers immediately took Water Bug into the bushes.

"Where did you take him?" Willow asked.

"I was showing him how to water the bushes, instead of his pants." They both laughed. "I think it is time he learned that."

"I do too. It would make things a lot easier."

"Two Feathers, do you know where we are? It all looks the same to me."

"Yes, I believe that we are not quite parallel with the mountain yet. We can't see it, because of the tall trees. I can climb up and look around, if you want me to."

As he climbed he said that he felt like a squirrel. He loved to hear her laugh. She didn't often.

"I can see the mountain. It is over there." He pointed. It looks strange and has smoke coming out of its side."

When he got down he suggested that they stay away from the mountain and continue in the trees until they were well past it.

"That is fine with me, and if you want to go a little farther today, we can. The horses have been grazing and we may find some water ahead for all of us to enjoy."

"Water Bug will whine if we put him back on Grandmother. I can hold him in front of me for a while." Two Feathers switched his bridle to the paint and scooped the boy up and slid on. The stallion is becoming a good mount, but I don't trust him well enough yet to take Water Bug on his back."

"I wondered why you switched. It is good to be cautious."

They rode along through the trees until Two Feathers signaled with his hand for Willow to come up beside him. He gently placed Water Bug on Lady in front of Willow. The boy was asleep. In one fluid motion, he placed an arrow in his bow and released it. Thirty yards away, a large deer toppled to the ground.

"That was amazing! I didn't see that deer. You are a good hunter. It didn't try to run away from us!"

"Some animals just seem curious about humans and they are not afraid."

Two Feathers cleaned the deer and struggled to put it on a horse's back.

"We really need to find a water hole soon. I think we should head back toward the mountain now"

"Lead the way," she said with a smile. It was getting late. The shadows were growing long, but they continued on. Finally when they stopped, they were still in the dense woods. They made a dry camp and sipped water from a jar in one of the packs.

Two Feathers was frowning.

"If we don't find water in the morning, we will have to back track to the stream by the mountain."

"We can't do that! The water is probably all hot now! We have to keep going ahead. We know the lake is close. We will find it." She was panicking.

"Willow, please calm down. You are right. We will find it." He could tell that she had endured all that she could. As he looked at her, tears began to flow down her face.

"I am sorry, but I can't go back to that mountain. Please don't ask me to go back near that mountain," she said. The tears were only the beginning of her body's betrayal. Her knees buckled and she collapsed into the leaves.

"Willow," he shouted, as he picked her up and carried her to the bundles laying her against them. Water Bug sensed that something was wrong. He whimpered and tried to crawl on her lap. Two Feathers picked him up, not knowing what to do next. She still hadn't opened her eyes. "What am I going to do? Great Spirit Lion of Judah help me," he called out loudly in anguish.

"Remember, I will be with you." Two Feathers wasn't sure if he had heard it or just thought it, but it helped him to become calm. He brought the jar of water near her and scooped some into a cup, sitting the boy on the ground, he handed it to him. Then, ever so

gently he patted water onto Willow's face and blew to make it colder. A soft groan escaped her lips just as she opened her eyes.

"What happened? What are you doing? She asked puzzled as he blew again onto the wet skin of her face and neck.

"You collapsed. Willow I am so sorry. I never should have left you there alone. I promise I will never leave you alone again. Somehow we will manage to stay together."

"Don't be silly. You can't hunt and do the things that men do, with a woman and baby in tow. I am fine now. I will finish setting up camp and get Bug fed and comfortable." She started to rise and found that the world was spinning around her.

"Maybe I better rest a few minutes more," she said settling back down.

"Willow, you need to sit there and I will get food for all of us. How are the burns on your feet? Do you want some grease to put on them?" He was trying to pretend that she was fine, and just the burns were the problem.

"My feet are much better. It helps to be riding. I am off them most of the time." Her head tipped back and jerked forward. She had dozed off for an instant. Why am I so sleepy? She wondered. Her head sought a place to rest and she was instantly sleeping soundly.

Two Feathers fed the boy and kept him busy until he started to suck his thumb. After a period of indecision, he decided it was best to leave her where she was. He tucked the blanket around her and then tied the cord to Water Bugs ankle and his own wrist.

"The hides aren't as cozy as the blanket, but we will make do, little man." Two Feathers curled around the boy snuggling with him until they all slept.

As soon as Water Bug stirred, Two Feathers carried him quietly into the bushes. Taking his hand, they went for a long walk to entertain him. Two Feathers pointed out a woodpecker and flowers, a squirrel and a rabbit while Willow continued to sleep.

By noon, Two Feathers knew that this was not just sleep. He could not wake her and her body was hot. I need to find that lake, so we have water. I need it to cool her and the horses need water, too, he worried. He made a travois, to transport her and packed up camp, quickly. Gently he placed her on the hide he had stretched and tied between two poles, covering her with the blanket. He fastened the device to be pulled by lady. She was smart and gentle. With Water Bug in front of him he started out carefully, not sure that she would be safe. The horses were strung out on a long rope. They followed along looking weary. They needed water.

When an idea came to him, a smile crossed his face for a moment as he considered it. If I let the stallion loose, he will go to water. We can follow his trail. If I lose him, it will be worth it, to have water for Willow.

As he removed the rope from the stallion, he opened the jar with a small bit of water in the bottom. He wet his hand and rubbed the horse's nose and lips.

"Find water for us boy. We need you to find the water." The horse took a step and then another. He seemed hesitant to leave the rest of the horses, and this man that had become his friend.

Suddenly he turned and headed swiftly through the trees and disappeared. I hope that I can follow him. Two Feathers face was a serious mask as he headed in the direction the stallion had gone.

He could hear the rumbling sound coming from the mountain in the distance, as he stopped to check Willow. He patted her face with water again and smeared grease on her cracking lips. Water Bug reached for the jar and drank nearly all that was left.

"I hope we find that lake soon, little Bug, or you and I are going to be as thirsty as the horses."

As they moved on, the horses seemed to be getting excited. They hurried along passing Two Feathers and causing a problem with the ropes. We must be getting near the water. They smell it. He hurried to keep pace; keeping one eye on the travois to make sure Willow was safe.

Suddenly, as they rounded a clump of dense trees, there it was, shining and beautiful. Releasing the ropes, he let the horses advance to the edge of the lake. There beside them stood the stallion. He blew a greeting and walked near Two Feathers and gave a snort.

"Good Boy, you did what I asked. You led us to the water. Thank you, Big Man." Two Feathers slipped a rope around the horse's neck but didn't tie it to anything. Like the others, he would enjoy walking in the edge of the water.

Water Bug was squirming in Two Feathers' arms wanting to be put down. Instead he was disappointed to be placed in his harness on Grandmother. He began to wail and squirm with indignation.

"Sorry little guy, but I know you are safe up there. I have to take care of Willow first." Gently he laid her on the wet sand. It was cool beneath her. As he cupped water on her hair and skin she opened her eyes.

"How are you feeling, Willow?" Willow sat up slowly, looking around.

"Where is the lion?"

"What lion?"

"The lion that brought me here, I was on his back and he said that he was taking me to the water."

"Willow, you were dreaming. I brought you here on that." Two Feathers pointed to the travois.

"I let the stallion loose and told him to find water. He led us here."

"Why is Water Bug crying? Why isn't he here by the water? He likes the water."

"Willow, you are still sick. I put him there to be safe. I can't just let him wade into this water. It is deep."

"Water Bug is crying. I must go to him."

"Stay there. Don't get up. I will bring him." Two Feathers was concerned. He knew that Willow was not thinking clearly. She seemed very strange. He brought Bug to her and helped her remove his clothing and then before he sat him near the edge of the water, he tied the cord to the boy's waist and around his own wrist. "There Bug, this is a bit more water than you are used to. What do you think of the lake?"

"Rain, water, drink, big drink," he said laughing with delight.

"Yes, the water is big," Willow said, looking in the distance as if she was seeing something fascinating.

Two Feathers looked in the direction she was.

At first he couldn't see anything that was that interesting and then his eyes focused on what appeared to be a horse with fire in its mane and tail. The sun was behind it glowing yellow through long red strands.

"I have never seen such a horse. It is magical. Look at the way it moves and prances."

The horse came closer as if to inspect new members of its royal court. It reared and challenged the black stallion, but Big Man backed away.

Next the "Fire Horse" approached the brown stallion. He also backed away. Two Feathers held his breath, waiting to see what it would do next. It nudged the mares each in turn as if counting them and snorted at the brown and white paint. Step by step it advanced until it stood near the water beside them. It had no fear. This horse acted as if it had ownership of the lake and all the land around it.

"Maybe he has never seen a human before. This lake must belong to him and his herd," said Two Feathers softly.

Willow was still very weak, but she slowly got to her feet and reached for the soft muzzle of the "Fire Horse". He stood perfectly still as she caressed him.

"You are magnificent," she breathed quietly. "You are king of this land. We will not take that from you. We ask only that you allow us to stay here this winter. We have no home. We need to find shelter before the snow comes." The horse nodded his head up and down as if he understood and then turned slowly to the direction he had come, giving a loud whinny. From between the rocks and trees poured horses of many colors but none like him.

Water Bug sat in the edge of the water staring up at him. He hadn't moved, but as he watched the many horses come down to the lake for a drink, he stood and took a step into the water, and then another. Soon it was above his waist. A tiny wave toppled him over and his head went under. Two Feathers jumped to the rescue and pulled him up, wiping the water from his face.

"That is enough water for now. I will get you some food."

He carried the boy up onto the grass away from the water, and horses, giving him a piece of meat to chew on. Willow followed unsteadily and sat beside Water Bug.

"How do you feel?" Two Feathers asked again. This time she answered.

"I feel tired and thirsty, but not dizzy anymore." Two Feathers hurried away and returned with the water pot freshly filled and a cup.

"Would you eat something?"

"No I am not hungry." After drinking a cup of water she dipped the cup full and handed it to Water Bug and then she lay back on the grass. She instantly had returned to the deep, unnatural sleep again. Two Feathers didn't know what he could do to help her, other than let her sleep. He placed his blanket in the shade and carried her to it. She didn't wake. Water Bug was rubbing his eyes and sucking his thumb.

"You need to sleep, too." Two Feathers laid the boy on the blanket and fastened the cord to the tree. "Once you are asleep, I am going to explore the rocks up there for a cave. It would be wonderful if we could find one here and not have to build a shelter. A cave would be better, less wind, and warmer when the winter cold comes." He stroked the boy's hair and watched his eyes close as he talked quietly.

The huge gray rocks loomed above the trees as Two Feathers entered their shade. At first he followed their base looking up, but knew that much of the face of the rocks was hidden from him by his position on the ground. Back farther he could see what appeared to be a dark area. I can't tell if that is a shadow or a cave, but I think I should climb up and look around. If it is a cave, it is going to be difficult to get there, he thought as he pulled himself up. It wasn't a cave, but just a deep shadow. As he turned to survey the area he could see Willow and Water Bug, asleep on the blanket. The Fire Horse stood near her as if on guard. I don't like him so close. What if he hurts her? He worried. He scrambled down to find that all the wild horses had left. The horses they had brought had remained, patiently waiting to have their packs removed.

I should have taken their packs off and tied them to a tree before the wild herd left. We could have lost all of them and our packs, too. I guess I'm not thinking clearly either. Two Feathers arranged the packs under the trees near Willow to make a wind break and started a small fire on the sand, circling it with rocks.

I wonder if there are fish in this lake. Two Feathers dropped his line in the water and waited. A fierce jerk let him know that his bait had been taken. The fish was large and he had trouble bringing it to the shore without a net. As it was baking, He made new racks to dry the deer meat. Water Bug woke Willow by crawling to her and patting her face. When Two Feathers looked at them, Willow was holding Bug on her lap and smiling at him. She got up and lifted the boy, seeming strong again. Two Feathers gave a sigh of relief, feeling that she was much better.

"That fish smells good. Water Bug likes fish."

"I will take him in the bushes," said Two Feathers. His pants are still dry.

When he returned he was telling Water Bug what a good boy he was.

"I wanted to start slicing the deer meat, but I can't find the bundle with the knives. We didn't leave it behind did we?"

"No, they are right there." They fed Water Bug, bites of fish while he played with pretty shells and polished stones they had found near the water. With the fire built up the meat would dry.

"I went up on the rocks as far as that point over there, but didn't find anything that could serve as a shelter yet. I will look farther over, tomorrow."

"You try hard to provide all that we need. I know that we will find something, and if we don't we can build a shelter back in the trees, where the wind is blocked by the rocks."

"Look at the lake, Willow. It is so still. The stars and moon can be seen on its surface. Do you think that we were brought here by the Lion Spirit?"

"Yes, I know he brought me. I rode on his back."

"Willow, I told you that was a dream."

For several days they searched the area hoping to find something that would serve as a shelter. None presented itself. Finally they chose a spot tucked between two huge boulders inside the tree line.

"It feels cozy here," offered Willow as they worked hard to cut several trees down with a small hatchet they had salvaged. It was difficult, time consuming work.

The trunks of four standing trees, stripped of the lower branches, anchored the corners. The walls and roof took form after several weeks of labor. They thatched the entire snug cabin with bundles of the tall grass that grew in patches along the shore.

"I was just thinking that it is strange that we haven't seen the fire horse since that first day," he said.

"I am sure that he is around. I can feel him watching us sometimes."

"Willow, I need to go hunting. Do you want to come or would you rather stay here near the shelter?"

"I will stay here. I think I will fish and see if I can catch some to dry for winter. Would you be able to set some snares before you go? I need rabbit pelts to make clothes for Water Bug."

She added wood to the small fire they had burning near their shelter. We will need a fire inside before long, she thought. That's what I will do today. I will start carrying stones inside to build a fireplace. Water Bug worked with her, carrying small rocks and not wandering off. He was helping in other ways, too. He had learned to stay dry and let them know when he needed to go behind the bushes. When they both tired of carrying rocks she cut soft, long needled pine branches and made beds along the back wall of the shelter. "These smell so nice, it will be easy to go to sleep laying on them," she said to the boy.

After lunch, they both curled up on the blanket on their new bed and napped. When Two Feathers returned, the camp was quiet. He had not been successful. He had not even found any prints of deer. He was worried. Quietly he entered the shelter and checked his sleeping family.

He stood outside looking up at the mountains towering in the distance. He wondered if they should travel farther along to the mountains he was seeing. It would be many days travel to reach them, but I could hunt along the way. Willow and Water Bug must come with me. She seems much better now, and we will have our shelter to come back to and I will make a safe, food cache up in a tree for our supplies before we leave.

Willow peeked out of the doorway.

"What are you looking at?" she asked. "Has the fire horse returned?"

"No, I was just looking at the mountains over there. There is flat grassland for part of the way and probably more woods. I wasn't able to find a deer today. Do you think you would be willing to ride with me to those mountains? I could hunt along the way. I want to see what is there."

"Who will take care of the food while we are gone? Animals will steal it."

"I need to make a cache up in one of the trees before winter anyway. I will do it before we leave. I noticed all the rocks you brought in the shelter. We can make a batch of mud to put the fireplace together and then that will be dry and ready for use when we come back, too."

"With this place here for us, when we return, the trip will seem like an adventure."

"Are you sure you are up to it? Are you feeling well now?"

"Yes, Two Feathers, I think it will be fun, and riding isn't hard work. Water Bug is learning to be a big boy now and he is easier to take care of. He has grown a lot in the last few months."

With their camp secure and their projects finished, they headed for the far mountains on their adventure, taking all their horses with them. Two Feathers rode the black stallion that he now called Friend.

"It is good that we were able to bring lots of water. With the smoked stomachs from the two deer we will be able to offer water to the horses, too, if we don't find any. Making a dry camp isn't as nice but at least we will have what we need," he said over his shoulder as they moved along.

After two days of travel they found a water hole surrounded by horse prints. "This must be one of the places that the Fire Horse brings his herd."

"I know it is."

"Willow, how can you be so sure? It could be other horses."

"Look over there, Two Feathers."

Back lit by the setting sun, he stood, once again appearing to have a mane and tail made of fire. Behind him stood his herd, all of them seemed to be waiting for the people to move away from their water hole.

"As soon as our horses finish drinking, I think we should move on. He hasn't given us any trouble so far and I don't want to anger him by invading his territory. We can camp over there under those trees."

"That is a good idea, Two Feathers. We need to respect his space."

They were riding in the foothills. They had not seen any game or tracks. Two Feathers was worried. Where have all the animals gone? He wondered. They stopped to rest and give Water Bug a chance to burn off a little energy. He ran up one hill and down another, with Willow close behind. She stopped him abruptly, clamping her hand over his mouth to quiet his laughter. Ahead were several women, bending over, gathering something from the grass and filling big baskets.

Cautiously she edged back to the horses. Two Feathers was nowhere in sight.

When he crept back his face was covered with sweat and frown wrinkles. Silently he scooped Water Bug into his arms and mounted the horse. Willow followed as they moved away, staying in between the hills, using them for cover.

"Where did you go? Water Bug nearly ran right over to those women."

"I climbed up on the rocks as far as I could just to look around. I spotted a big village farther back between the hills. They have a large herd of horses, and many cooking fires. They aren't the raiders, but they aren't people we know either.

"I was close enough to hear the women talking, but I couldn't understand them. Two Feathers, they were gathering nuts. I studied the trees they were under, and on the way back we should see if we can find some."

"Nuts would be good to have this winter, but right now I want to put as much distance between them and us as we can before it gets dark."

They hurried along, with Water Bug complaining all the way. Willow rode beside him later as he finally slowed the pace. "Two Feathers, why did you react that way? We can't understand them, but if we stayed with them, we could learn their language. You must not mistrust everyone we come across or we will never find people we can live with."

"I don't want to live with anyone else. We are a people. We must remember the people of our village. If we join someone else's village, we will become one of them and our people will be lost forever."

"Two Feathers, we will never forget our families or our village, but we do need to find a village that we can join. In the spring, we must look for other people from our summer council meeting. They too will remember our people, and they will help us to survive."

He was silent and stone faced. She could see that he didn't agree at all.

"Father, help him to see the wisdom in joining with others. He is young and so am I. Can we raise Water Bug all by ourselves? There is so much that we need to learn. She prayed silently.

"Thank you for giving my strength back and for helping us to build the shelter. We will not freeze this winter. Help me to recognize other foods that I can gather for us, and show me where the nut trees are." She laughed to herself.

"I hope you don't mind me bothering you with such simple things as nut trees," she added.

The weather turned chilly at night and they were happy to have the finished fireplace to use.

One evening Two Feathers raced in the shelter excited.

"I found deer tracks! Big ones! There are several traveling together. Tomorrow I am going hunting. They all seemed to be gone for a while. The mountain rumbling and the fire frightened them. I am glad they are back."

"While you are hunting, I think I will take Water Bug and look for a nut tree."

"Just be careful. I don't want you two to get lost," he warned laughing.

"I won't. I will finish this mat to take. I made it while waiting by the clearing. It just needs the sides stitched to turn it into a big pouch, like the ones we used for the corn. You will see, Two Feathers. God will fill it for us."

CHAPTER EIGHT
A GIFT

As the days grew colder, they were glad to have rabbit stew. The snares were working and soon Water Bug was dressed in warm clothes. He had learned to stay away from the lake, but Willow still watched him vigilantly. Two Feathers had gotten another deer and one day he came back with an antelope. Willow wasn't sure that this was an animal she would eat, but she liked the hide. Stripped of its harsh quill-like coat it would make a warm shirt-dress for her. For Two Feathers, they had made a deer skin shirt and pants. None of them had a coat or boots and their bedding was minimal. They dragged their sleeping hides nearer the warmth of the fire.

Willow felt like winter was lasting forever. Weeks of bitter cold went by. It was so cold that they could not go out for more than a few minutes to gather wood. Their diet kept them alive, but the cold sapped their fat reserves. By spring they were thinner and lacked energy. Even on sunny days Willow preferred to sit inside, until one day she heard voices.

"Two Feathers wake up! Listen. I hear people talking and laughing."

Cautiously they watched from behind the trees. People were scattered along the shore, untangling huge nets. They were preparing to enter the water with them. Others were setting up temporary shelters or starting cooking fires. Huge stacks of baskets were being unloaded from the backs of packhorses. An entire village had appeared on the shore of the lake. Grandmothers cuddled babies, while mothers prepared

105

pots of food. Men stripped to minimal clothing and shrieked with laughter as they pulled the nets out into the cold water of the lake. Children ran along the sand, gathering shells and shouting to each other. It seemed they were all having a wonderful time. The nets were weighted and left in the water. The women scoured the area diligently for new spring greens. Willow strained to see what they were picking, as they gathered food for the evening meal.

The nets were slowly brought to shore the next day, yielding basket after basket of fish. Once they were cleaned, the large fish were hung on lines above the fires to dry and be preserved by the smoke.

Two Feathers insisted that they stay in the cover of the trees and remain hidden. Willow wanted to run out and meet these people. They all seemed happy and kind even if she couldn't understand them. She was eager for female companionship. She had so much to learn.

Finally they became sure that this was the people of the village they had discovered in the foothills of the mountains.

"This must be something they do every year as soon as winter breaks. They come for the fish and new greens and enjoy getting out after a long winter."

The villagers stayed three nights and left the fourth morning, with their baskets bulging with smoked fish. Many that rode there would now have to walk home. There horses carried packs and heavy baskets. Willow was sad when they left. Two Feathers was just relieved. He had barely slept the entire time they were there.

As the last villager walked away in the long procession, Willow stepped out to watch them disappear in the distant grasslands. Near their door, sat a basket filled with dry fish. A net, clean and folded lay beside it and on top of it was a smaller basket with several bunches of different greens, each tied with a cord. In the bottom was a pretty hair comb made from a shell.

"Two Feathers look! They knew that we were here. They left us a gift!"

"I wonder how they knew we were here. Someone must have discovered our shelter when they were gathering wood. I wonder why they left us alone."

"When we didn't come out, they probably thought that we didn't want to be friends. They must have seen us watching them. They knew that I was trying to see what greens they picked. Look they made little samples for me. They even left me a hair comb." Willow felt like she had lost a precious opportunity.

"We have to go after them! We have to explain to them somehow," she cried.

"No! It is better this way. We will be gone soon. We won't be here when they come back."

"Why? Why won't you meet them? They are nice people!"

Two Feathers didn't answer. He turned and walked to the tree where he had built the food cache. One by one he lowered the remaining packs.

"We leave at first light," he said, offering no explanation.

It was very early in the season. The ground was still frozen in a few places where the dense shade screened the ground from the sun. He hoped to travel far enough south, fast enough, to find a place they could plant their seed corn and spend the summer. As soon as it was harvested, he thought they could travel again, farther south until cold weather. Now that he had built a shelter, he knew he could do it again, if they didn't find a cave or someplace suitable.

Two Feathers felt guilty for making the decision to immediately move on without discussing it with Willow. He had promised her that he would never make her go anywhere. Now he had stopped her from trying to make friends and had announced that they would leave in the morning. He knew that she liked it here and that if they stayed, next winter would be better. They would have all summer to gather hides for more clothing. They could plant the corn on the edge of the grassland. The soil was good there. No, he thought. We need to head south and look for... What am I looking for? Few people will speak our language.

Then he admitted to himself that he wanted to find the raiders! If I find them, what will I do? I am just one against many. If our entire village could not stand against them, how can I? I must never put Willow and Water Bug in danger. I need to think. If we knew where the raiders were and knew their language. It would be a lot easier. Maybe I should go alone, but I promised I would not leave her alone again. We could plant the corn here and that would give me all summer to search for their camp, and then I could come back to harvest the corn and we could travel then. If I tell her the truth she will never agree. If I lie to her, she will know. I don't know what to do, but I know I cannot leave this territory without avenging our village!

When he looked up, movement caught his eye. It was the Spirit Lion. He came slowly and stood before him.

"Vengeance is mine. It is not your work. You have other responsibilities. When you do what you should, you will find joy and peace. Do not be troubled. Know that I am with you."

Two Feathers returned to the shelter to find it empty. Willow had taken Water Bug to the lake. They sat on the sand tossing small stones into the water and talking quietly. He could see them but couldn't hear what they were saying.

When a stone made a large splash near them, they both turned around.

"May I join your game?"

"Of course, Two Feathers, but don't you have things to get ready if you plan on us leaving in the morning?" Her voice was strained. It was obvious that she was upset and offended.

"Willow, please forgive me. I should not have stopped you from trying to talk to those people, if that was really what you wanted to do. I have no right to force my will on you. We don't have to leave tomorrow or any day unless you want to."

"Thank you Two Feathers. I still would like to leave, but to try to find people from the summer council. Do you think you could find the place where it is held?"

"I think so, but I am not sure. Maybe if we both talk about what we saw along the way, we can piece it together and find the route our people took."

"Oh, Two Feathers, do you mean it? Are you willing to try?"

"Yes, I am and if we leave now, we can find a place near there to plant the corn. "

Water Bug wasn't sure what they were discussing, but he wanted to be included. He crawled on Willow's lap just as she excitedly hugged Two Feathers. Water Bug was squashed between them. He was laughing.

They left very early the next morning, with more bundles than they had brought. Food was not a problem now that she was sure which greens were safe to eat. They headed straight through the burned forest and hurried past the mountain without stopping.

They spent one night at their shelter near the clearing. They were surprised to see that it had weathered well.

They reached the campsite of their people and skirted it continuing on without stopping. They followed the little stream until it disappeared in a basin of rocks and shrubs.

"I can remember passing this way. I think it was five or six years ago, when we went to the summer council. I am not sure which way we went from here."

"Yes, we were both very young. I can remember heading out toward the morning sun. It was early and it shone in our eyes. Remember?"

"Yes, you are right, and my mother lifted me up on the back of my father's horse because she said I walked too slowly. That day I didn't see much until we were past it. But I do remember we stopped to camp one night in grass that went on forever. It was nearly as tall as the people, and on the way back it had grown to reach over my father on horseback."

"We are traveling earlier in the year, so the grass won't look the same, but I think we are on the right route." Two Feathers tried hard to remember, but he had been walking with other boys near his age and they had teased, played and tussled much of the way. He didn't want to admit it to Willow; but he had not really paid much attention to the route.

As she had suggested earlier, the grass seemed to go on forever. Finally they stopped to rest, giving the horses water they were carrying. Their meal was food she had prepared the night before. No fire was needed. They tromped the grass down in a circle and spread their hides. Water Bug was tired from traveling and fell asleep as soon as he had eaten. Willow had started to trust him to stay near at the shelter by the lake, but here in a sea of grass taller than he was, she felt that she needed to use the cord again to be sure he didn't wander away and get lost. The night was cold and clear. They had to use the blanket and hides to cover themselves. Two Feathers had hobbled their horses. He knew they would not go far. They had all the grass they could want, right in front of them.

"Good morning Willow. Just as you said, the sun is shining in our eyes. The land here is flat and has no trees to block it." Willow tipped her face up, glad to receive the warmth.

"I think it feels good on my skin. It was cold last night. I am sure that we are heading south."

"Look there is a big oak tree. I can remember there were lots along the way. My friends and I would play games, throwing the acorns to see who threw the farthest."

"It sounds like the boys had more fun than the girls. Our mothers always made us stay near them. I can remember her constantly saying,

"Hurry along and keep up."

"I will be glad when we get out of this grass. I like having lots of trees around me. It feels like we are vulnerable here."

"That's what I was thinking. I feel the same way," he admitted. "Look over there. Do you remember that big gray rock? It looks out of place here. There aren't any others. I think that we climbed it and I can't quite recall, but I think the Chief told us to stay on the trail and not to climb any more rocks. I was glad that I was off it when he rode up."

His mind had stored small landmarks, that were helpful and reassuring that they were heading the right way.

"Didn't we travel beside a river for most of a morning?"

"I think it is ahead. See that tree line. We can camp there tonight."

He said.

"The horses will like that as much as we will." As the day wore on, the trees seemed to recede.

"We don't seem to be getting any closer. Let's stop for a few minutes and give Water Bug and the horses a break," she suggested.

"I have to say that I am tired of riding, too," Two Feathers admitted.

When they finally found the Hickory, they watched for a place to swim and relax. Two Feathers took Water Bug into the water and they played until their fingers were wrinkled.

With a campfire going, they sat close together while Willow made fresh corn cakes and cooked young dandelion greens and boiled some of the dried meat. Water Bug gagged and refused to eat the greens. He had never had them and would have to develop a taste for them. They slept under the trees and once again, Willow used the cord to give her mind an assurance that Water Bug was safe.

In the morning, they moved out following the river until it curved sharply to the right and flowed into the forest. They continued on straight.

"I remember all these big beautiful trees. There is an opening ahead."

"Isn't that where one of the hunters got a deer? We should go quietly. Maybe we can have fresh meat for our evening meal." They moved forward slowly, walking the horses.

"Twang" went his bow, and the arrow hit its mark. We won't have deer but we can have a fresh rabbit."

Willow laughed as she slid from her horse.

"That was a good shot. He was fast!"

As they removed the packs and set up camp, Willow could feel a gentle calm enter her being.

"Two Feathers, how far do you think we are from the location of the summer camp?"

"I'm not sure, but it can't be more than another days ride. I think we are getting close."

"If we find that little stream in the morning, we will know that we are very close. We should stop there and plant the corn. It would be a good location to watch for people coming to the meeting."

"Do you think we should go a little farther? We might be able to camp there tonight."

"That is fine with me, but Water Bug is already starting to whine. He is hungry and tired of riding."

"If we go a little farther and don't find it, we will stop. I know that he will love that little stream. It is like the one back home." They quickly replaced the few packs they had removed and moved on, after handing Water Bug a cup of water and piece of softened meat.

They had been right. The stream was only a few minutes ahead. Water bug's face was lit by a big smile when he saw the stream. His feet were hurrying to the water before his clothes were pulled off.

"Wait just a minute Bug. I don't want you to get your clothes all wet." He struggled to pull his arms from the shirt. The water was very cold, but it didn't stop him from plopping down in it.

"That is the happiest he has been since we left our village. I think the lake was just too much water. It scared him a little."

"The stream is very cold. We can't leave him in there very long. If you will get a fire going we will be able to get him dry and warm near it."

Two Feathers felt happy. Things had gone the way they had planned. As he removed the horse's packs and hobbled them, he found himself trying to decide where he could work up the sod to plant corn.

"This is a good place to spend the summer. We can choose a place for the corn and camp here under the trees," he said.

"I like it here. You will be able to hunt here, too. The deer are in this area. We know that." The rabbit stew contained nothing but corn and rabbit meat, with a handful of cattail root pounded and added to thicken it, but they enjoyed it.

As days passed, they struggled in the heavy sod to clear the ground for the corn. Two days after they had planted it, it started to rain and rained all night.

"That was a blessing. We needed a rain to start the corn growing," said Willow.

"Yes but we need a shelter. I don't like trying to sleep, huddled under hides, trying to keep our supplies dry. Where would you like me to build it?"

"Anywhere, here in the shade will be fine. Now that the corn is in the ground, there isn't much for us to do this summer, but hunt, process the meat and make clothes from the hides," she said.

"Eventually, we will have all the clothes that we need and we will be able to start collecting hides for a nice tent."

Nearly four months later, Willow found that she was trembling as she saw a slow column of people making their way through the prairie grass toward the stream and their camp. At the head of the column three men rode. On the left was Flying Eagle, a young, strong warrior. On the right, Growling Bear, a seasoned warrior with the look of wisdom and experience. They guarded the gray haired, leather-faced Chief.

Everything about him gave an air of authority, from the best quality mount, in pure white, to the multicolored beadwork on his knee high boots. His open shirt was fringed in fur and his hair was braided with beads and feathers. On his chest rested a heavy breast plate made of blue turquoise stones and beads of silver and bone. His horse was bridled in soft brown leather adorned with silver and turquoise medallions. The heavily padded leather saddle was tooled and resting on a deep burgundy blanket, fringed with white bone and silver beads. She couldn't take her eyes from him.

Finally she realized that he had stopped directly in front of her and was looking at her in a curious way.

"Girl, what people have arrived from this direction, ahead of the Blue Stone People? And why do you camp here and not at the summer camp grounds?"

Willow's mouth was frozen. She was so awestruck that she couldn't speak. Two Feathers stepped out of their shelter in time to save her from further embarrassment.

"We are here from the north to visit friends. I am Two Feathers, this is my sister, Willow and the little one is Water Bug, My Chief. We have not yet entered camp, but no other people have come this way. Perhaps others have arrived but from the east or south."

"Thank you, my son; we will meet again in camp. It is good," said the Chief as he crossed the stream slowly so that there was not a splash to stain his beautiful boots. He intended to make a grand entrance with his people and wanted his appearance to be flawless. He was pleased with the young hunter's answer. They had arrived with perfect timing. Most of the camps were already set up along the east or south side of the circle. The Blue Stone People had the space to the Northwest. He was glad that each morning the sun would light his white horse and large tent decorated with a large, yellow ocher stained sun. It would remind all those present of his authority and power.

The Blue Stone People continued to move on, most did not observe Willow or her shelter. Some smiled; others were talking excitedly and didn't notice the thin girl standing in the shade. They all seem nice enough, she thought. I think they are very blessed. They have many packhorses and everyone has a horse to ride. I noticed that every one of their people wore a necklace with blue stones on it.

We are blessed, too, she thought. We have many horses. Two Feathers had held Water Bug in his arms watching the parade of people on horses until the boy became restless. So many people, he thought.

"I wonder how far they have come."

That evening as Willow and Two Feathers sat beside their small fire, they talked about the Chief of the Blue Stone People and how well they all were dressed and the fact that even small children had a horse to ride.

"These people must have been here when we were here before, but I don't remember them. Do you?" He was frowning as he asked.

"No, I don't know if I will actually remember anyone here. I was young and kept close to my mother all the time. I think she was afraid that she would lose me."

"I may be able to spot some of the young men that were in the same games with me. I hope so. It will make it easier, if we see someone that we know."

"Do you think it would be alright if we just trail in and look around? There are so many people at these meetings. Do you think that anyone will know that our people are the ones that are not here? Eventually we will have to find the Council Chief, and tell him what has happened to our people, but I don't want to do that until we have had a chance to decide which of the villages we would like to go back with for the winter. That way we will be able to request to be accepted by them at the same time."

The next morning, after carefully watering every hill of their corn, and fastening their food supplies high in a tree, Two Feathers, Willow and Water Bug prepared to follow the trail left by the Blue Stone People. They wanted to take all their horses, fearing that something might happen to any they left behind hobbled. In a moment of whimsy, Willow painted a white lion on each of the shoulders of the black stallion, and insisted that Two Feathers spread his blanket on the horse's back to ride on. She painted the same lion on each of their horses, knowing that it would make it easier to recognize them. There would be many beautiful horses. She mixed another batch of chalk and grease and used it to decorate the edges of two of their hides.

"Now," she said, "It is your turn. If you will sit here where I can reach your hair, I will do my best to braid it smoothly and put your feathers in. Her first try was not as nice as she wanted it. She took it out and tried again. When the braid was finished, she pulled it tightly back and folded it into a bar at the back of his head and wrapped it together with a strip of rabbit's fur to secure it. The last thing she did was to firmly press the bone clip holding the two eagle feathers, into the top of his braid. "You look handsome," she said, admiring her handy work.

"Thank you Willow, I have something for you to wear." He had repaired the chain and her mother's cross could be worn. He slipped it over her head and watched as her eyes filled with tears. "Please don't cry. She is always with you. I took this from one of the packs and have been working on it. It is a very hard substance and it took a longtime but I made a hole in the top of your crystal. You can use this thin strip of leather to fasten it on your neck. No one will have a necklace like yours."

Willow smiled as he tied the crystal so that it would rest below the cross. She placed her hand on her chest to feel the cross and the shape of the crystal.

"Both of these are special to me, for different reasons. Thank you for fixing them so that I can wear them. Now I need to fix my hair so that we can leave. She pulled her heavy black hair to the right side of her head and made one thick braid, tying the end with many wraps of a strip of rabbit fur. On the opposite side of her head, she inserted first her mother's silver hair comb and then the shell comb. It gave the appearance of one thick comb. Next she wrapped thin strips of rabbit fur around each ankle and crossed them on her calves knotting them in front just below her knees.

Sitting in the shade, waiting for this day, Willow had made a skirt. The fur peeked out here and there, from the fringe on it. "Now it looks as if I am barefoot by choice. They won't think that I don't have moccasins. "I don't want to look needy," she said, "or people will not want us."

"You look beautiful, and I think the idea of painting the lions on our horses is a good one. You are very talented. It will make people wonder," he said smiling. "What can we do for Water Bug?"

"He is fine. He is clean and his clothes are, too. I wonder if his hair is long enough for a little braid. Let's try. Hold him still for me." Once the rabbit fur was tied to hold the short braid in place, he shook his head to feel his braid and the fur move back and forth on his neck. "Leave it alone and don't do that Water Bug or you will shake the braid out."

Two Feathers laughed.

"If he keeps doing that, people will think there is something wrong with him." Then they both laughed.

"I have this pack ready with things to keep him satisfied. I think we can go."

"I am ready," said Two Feathers, lifting Water Bug up on Grandmother. He fastened him in his harness. Beneath him rested one of the decorated hides. The small pack was placed on lady and the second decorated hide was for Willow to ride on. They made an interesting group as they entered the council area. Some turned their heads, but only a few greeted them or smiled. Everyone seemed too busy to pay attention to them, until a man stepped in front of Two Feathers, taking hold of his bridle.

"I greet you, my son and daughter. Where are you from?"

"North," stammered Two Feathers.

"We have all been wondering if your people would come this year. Your space is a fine one, there under the trees. You have water further back for the horses. When will your Chief arrive? Why are you ahead of him?"

"I have news of him and our people. I must speak immediately to the Chief of the Council," said Two Feathers. "I have an important message for him."

"Chief Dark Wolf of the Blue Stone People is Chief of the Council, but you can't see him right now. He is with the Chief of the Omati, in his tent. They are having a meeting with several other Leaders. You must wait."

"We will take care of our horses and then perhaps by then he will have time to speak to me." The man nodded and directed them to walk the horses around behind several tents, to avoid the many people walking around.

"I forgot that each village has an assigned location by the direction they live from the council meeting. Our people have been missed. We must tell Chief Dark Wolf what has happened."

Willow was not eager to enter the tent of Chief Dark wolf when the time came. He and his towering tent intimidated her. Two Feathers entered when he was finally invited. They had waited outside for nearly an hour.

"My Chief, I bring serious news of a dreadful nature. The village in the north of the Sentu is no more. All of our people travel in the spirit world. We are the only ones left. We are Willow, Water Bug, and I am Two Feathers."

CHAPTER NINE
THE SUMMER COUNCIL

"One moon before the moon of harvest, raiders came riding out of the morning sun. They killed everyone except two women, which they took with them. One was Water Bug's mother. The other was a cousin to Willow. They also took our Chief away from camp and tied him in a tree where they tortured him until he died. I was out of camp on my three-day journey or I too would be dead. When I returned, I found Willow and Water Bug hiding in the stream beneath a willow tree. She has cared for the boy since then, and has been a good mother to him. She is young, but she works very hard.

The raiders burned all the tents and destroyed everything they could. They took many of our horses. We found some scattered and were able to catch them. We have seven now."

Chief Dark Wolf nodded. His face was solemn.

"Please continue my son."

"That first morning, we used a horse to drag dead trees to the center of our camp. Together, she and I carried the bodies of our people and placed them on the wood. We had to make two fires. It was ghastly work. We kept them burning for four days and nights. On the fifth day I dug a hole and buried all the bones in the center of the camp. We knew that our Chief was absent, but I learned his fate later when I was riding one of the horses we had caught. I discovered the raiders camped not far from our village. I worried that they might return because of the big fires we had lit, but they didn't." Two Feathers continued.

"After the corn was ready we harvested it and left the village, taking dried deer meat, and a few things we were able to salvage. I returned from my vision quest on the paint. He is mine. He is strong. He carried me and was able to bring the deer that I shot, too."

Two Feathers knew that he sounded prideful, but he wanted this Chief to know that he was a good hunter.

Once the story had been told, Two Feathers' shoulders drooped. He felt such relief that he had to fight back tears. All these months he had been doing his best to recover, but he had not had an opportunity to tell anyone what they had been through. Chief Dark Wolf stood beside the youth for a moment, silently.

"Where is Willow and Water Bug?"

"They are outside waiting, my Chief."

Chief Dark Wolf stepped to the doorway and looked out.

"Willow, Please come in," he said in a kind voice. He was deeply moved by the story that Two Feathers had related.

"I am grieved by the loss of your people, the Sentu. They were your people and mine. Many of the families here were joined to families in your camp. Please stay here. I will return soon." Chief Dark Wolf's face reflected his shock and loss as he stepped out into the bright sunshine. Moonflower, his wife, was not in sight. Snow Star, his married daughter, wife of Flying Eagle, stood with a group of young mothers talking under the trees, and watching their little ones play in the shade.

"Snow Star, where is your mother?" She was startled by his abrupt approach and question.

"I am not sure, Father, but I saw her earlier walking with Morning Dove and some other women toward the stream."

"Please find her for me and tell her to come to our tent. I need her."

"Yes father."

"Snow Star, you can leave Watching Owl here. He is having fun. I will watch him for you until you get back," said one of the women.

"Thank you," she said over her shoulder as she hurried away. She felt apprehension. Snow Star had never seen her father look like that before. She knew that something very serious must have happened. She raced through the trees, nearly bumping people as she darted this way and that, quickly asking if they had seen Moonflower.

When she finally located her, Moonflower was relaxing, sitting on the bank of the steam, with her feet in the water. Several women were there doing the same while visiting with her.

"I am sorry mother to interrupt you, but Father needs you to come quickly." Moonflower could tell by the tone of her daughter's voice that this was no trivial request. She pushed herself up and struggled to step into her moccasins with wet feet.

"Where is he?"

"He said to come to the tent." Moonflower moved quickly across the camps central area with Snow Star right beside her.

"Mother, what could have happened?"

Moonflower rushed to the tent and Snow Star followed.

"What has happened?" she asked, forgetting her manners.

"Moonflower, this is Two Feathers, Willow and Water Bug, of the Sentu. This is Moonflower, my wife and my daughter Snow Star," he said, keeping the introductions short and not giving anyone else a chance to speak.

"Two Feathers has brought word of a terrible raid on the camp of the Sentu. All were killed except these three children."

"My Chief, I have returned from my three day journey with a large deer. I am a hunter. I have changed my own name and that of the girl and child. Willow and I have buried our entire village. The Sentu, are no more. We are The People of the Lion. We have survived the winter with our own hard work. We have cared for the boy and he grows in size and knowledge. We are not children. We ask that you acknowledge us as a family."

"Two Feathers, you and Willow have done well. I need time to think about all that you have told me. Moonflower and I welcome you to our tent. You may stay here with us for the rest of the summer meeting." He stepped out quickly and headed for the tent of his friend, Chief Black Thorn, the Chief of the Omati.

Snow star embraced Willow and began to talk with her. Moonflower immediately offered food and tea.

"I can't imagine how you managed to care for the boy. It must have been very difficult. I have a boy just a bit bigger and even with my mother's help sometimes I get very tired."

"Where is your son now?" asked Willow.

"The women are watching him over there under the trees. Please let me carry Water Bug for you and I will introduce you to my friends."

"Thank you, but he doesn't need to be carried. I will hold his hand and he will walk." Moonflower followed along handing a cracker to the boy to nibble.

"Everyone, this is Willow and Water Bug. They will be staying in our tent during the council." Snow Star picked up Watching Owl to show him to Willow, but he immediately began to whine squirm to get back down. He wanted to see Water Bug.

"Thank you for watching him for me. I think he needs a lunch and his nap." The women each talked with Willow, and somehow they managed to keep their curiosity in check. Moonflower smiled and suggested that they should give the boy some lunch and see if he would rest.

"I will put him on a hide under the trees. After a little food and a cup of sweet tea, he lay beside her with his thumb in his mouth but it took a long while for him to sleep in the new environment with so many people and their sounds.

As usual, she put the cord on his ankle but this time she fastened it to the tree. She wanted to be able to move a distance away to talk to Moonflower without waking him.

Two Feathers left the tent and the women to visit. He wanted to find some of the young men from the last council meeting. He saw a group of young men laughing and talking as they carried wood for the community fire. As he joined them, the conversation stopped.

"Hello Teewah, one of them said. I remember you from a long time ago. You beat me in a race! We were very young then, about six or seven, I think."

"I remember your faces but only a couple names," he said as he greeted all of them.

"My name is now Two Feathers. I have completed my journey."

"My name is now Bear Paw, and this is Gray Squirrel."

"Hello again, my name is Spotted Feather. I was given that name after my journey. I was looking around and didn't see your people from the north. Their space is still unused. Aren't they coming?"

"No, said Two Feathers sadly. "Their spirits are gone, to the other world. There was a raid. All were killed, except a girl, Willow, a little boy, Water Bug, and me."

"You lost all your people? How did you survive?"

"We just did. We worked and took each day as a new beginning. We took new names and have decided to call ourselves, "The People of the Lion."

"That is amazing and terrible at the same time. Where is Willow? Is she to be your wife?"

"We have not thought of such things. She has been my sister. But she does all the work that a wife would do and has been a mother to Water Bug."

"Who were the raiders?" asked Bear Paw.

"I don't know. I kept one of the arrows to show the Council Chief, but I left it at our camp. I will have to ride back to get it."

"We will go with you if you want. The games won't start until tomorrow."

"I will tell Willow that I am leaving and then we can go."

"He says she is not his wife," offered Gray Squirrel. They all laughed.

"While you go tell her; we better pile some more wood for the fire. Come get us when you are ready."

"It is good," said Two Feathers as he strolled in the direction of Chief Dark Wolf's tent. He found Willow with Moonflower, sitting in the shade near the napping boy. Water Bug slept soundly. Two Feathers politely nodded to Moonflower.

"Willow, I will be riding out to our camp with some others. I will return soon. Is there anything there that you would like me to bring back?"

"No, I think we have everything that we need for now." Before she could ask him why he was going, he had turned and walked quickly toward the horses. After patting the rump of each horse and giving them some attention, He slid up onto his paint, Patches, knowing that he could trust the horse to walk carefully through the noise and confusion without becoming agitated. As he circled around, behind the tents, he could see the others waiting for him. He waved at them and headed through the trees at the edge of camp where they had entered. The others rode following Two Feathers, eager for any adventure that would take them out of the din of so many people.

*****

Moonflower had lowered her heavy body to the grass beside Willow, heaving a deep sigh, not so much from the effort as from the sad ache in her heart as the reality sunk in that she would never see her friends and family from the camp of the Sentu again. She had felt something was wrong. A sense of sad loss had bothered her all winter, but she couldn't explain it. Here at the camp she was sure that something dreadful had happened when the Sentu were so late and hadn't arrived. The Sentu had to travel the farthest and because of that they usually got to the summer camp days before the Blue Stone people. The last half of their journey marked the trail for the Blue Stone People. She was sure they would come this year. It was the seventh year.

"Willow you are welcome here with us. There are many people among our village that will be eager to have you join them."

"Thank you, Moonflower, but we wish to remain a family of our own. Two Feathers has chosen the name for us. We are "The People of the Lion of Judah," but we need to be near other people right now so that we can learn more skills. I was just learning to weave when the raiders came."

"You will enjoy meeting my friend, Morning Dove. She taught Brave Sparrow how to weave. Brave Sparrow is my adopted daughter. She has changed her name to Sarah of the Blue Stone People."

"Why did she change her name?"

"That is a story for another day, Willow. Here comes Morning Dove. You can meet her now."

"Hello Moonflower, you have settled quickly. You are better organized than I am. Who is this pretty young lady?"

"Morning Dove, I would like you to meet Willow, of the Sentu and now of The People of the Lion. She is staying with us."

"It is nice to meet you, Willow."

"Moonflower said that you are an excellent weaver and perhaps would teach me. I have much to learn before I can be a good mother to Water Bug."

"Who is Water Bug," she asked.

"He is there sleeping. I am his mother now, since the raid on the Sentu."

"What raid? What are you talking about?"

"Raiders rode out of the morning sun and killed the entire village. Only three people were left, Water Bug, Two Feathers and me. They burned all the tents and destroyed all they could. They took two of our women. One was Water Bug's mother. I held him in the water under willow brush. They didn't find us."

"How long ago was it?" asked Moonflower.

"It was last summer. We waited until the corn was ripe and harvested it. Two Feathers is a good hunter. We always had something to eat. We went north of the mountains and built a shelter. That is where we spent the winter."

"You were very brave and strong to have survived everything. I hope that you and Two Feathers will be able to choose a new people to live with. You should not have to live alone," said Moonflower.

"Thank you. You are kind."

*****

Two Feathers greeted his friends as they rode out together.

"You look like you are all ready for a hunt. I brought my bow, too. I don't like being without it."

As they rode along, Bear Paw introduced Debon.

"His people have a similar story to yours, Two Feathers. Six Abalinah joined us a year ago, Debon, and his brothers, Kier, and Hondor. His brothers are married and brought their wives, but they brought one woman that isn't married. Her name is Sheltah. The Blue Stone People are prosperous. You should follow us, Two Feathers."

When they splashed across the little stream and entered Two Feather's camp, He looked up to see a line of dust on the horizon.

"I think we may be in great good luck. There is enough dust there above the grass to be a small herd of buffalo."

"Let's go see," said Two Feathers.

They rode out in the direction of the dust line. All of them were thinking they would love to take part in a buffalo hunt and be given credit for providing the entire Summer Council with a feast.

As they rode closer, Two Feathers was the first to slow his horse and finally stop.

"It is not buffalo. It is riders. Many riders and they come swiftly." He formed a tube with both hands and placed it to his eye so he could see more clearly.

"They wear war paint. Hurry, we must warn the people. They must not be caught unprepared."

Two Feathers, grabbed the arrow from his camp as he passed. The feeling in the pit of his stomach told him that all too soon he would have more just like it. The young men broke the rules when they rode hazardously through the people as they raced to the Council Chief's tent.

"Raiders come from the west, my Chief," he shouted as they dismounted and entered the tent without being invited.

"We saw many riders coming swiftly. They are wearing war paint and right behind us. We came to warn you."

"You have done well. Spread the word so the warriors can arm themselves before the attack." The Chief sent two of the young men to ride through the surrounding area to warn the women and children so they would gather in the woods behind the far tents. Women grabbed their babies and ran to comply with the Chief's instruction. Children were crying as their mothers pulled them hastily through vines and bushes, into the dense woods.

The men took up arms forming lines of defense near the little stream.

The raiders came, thundering toward the stream with reckless abandon, shrieking and yelling their battle cries. The warriors of the people at the council had swiftly taken the few minutes of warning to prepare wisely. They had lined the creek with men. Each chose his position well. The next line of defense was just inside the large area of the summer meeting. A line of men had stationed themselves at the back of the tents. The raiders would have to ride through both lines to reach the center of the camp.

Two Feathers ran to find Willow and Water Bug, but he didn't have to go very far. Willow had grabbed the boy and was heading through their horses straight for the water behind the open space that would have held the camp of the Sentu. In her mind, the water offered protection.

"Willow," he shouted, "Wait a second." His arms wrapped around her in the only hug of affection he had ever given her.

"Hide as you did before. You will be safer if you stay out of sight and we both know Bug will be quiet as long as he has water to play in. Don't watch what is happening. You have enough bad memories. I will come find you when it is over. I love you Willow. You and Bug are my family now."

He ran to join the line of defense that was forming in the center of the camp. In his mind he heard the words. *"J am always with you."*

"Lion of Judah, help us to protect these people." He really didn't understand the power in those words, but he believed that the Lion would help. His hand sought his spirit bag, remembering the tuft of lion hair in it.

The vicious raid was over quickly. The raiders were obviously outnumbered, but the losses of the people were many. Two Feathers leapt on the back of the barbaric appearing raider, riding on him as he pulled his knife. Two Feathers was clearly much younger and thinner than the man he had attacked. Two Feathers raised his knife and held it tightly against the throat of the man as the raider slid slowly to his knees. Three raiders were captured alive and held prisoner. Everyone wanted an answer to the same questions. Where had they come from and why had they so savagely attacked the people?

As soon as Two Feathers was able to release his captive to the warriors that surrounded him, he ran to find Willow.

The camp lay silent only for a moment, before the women found their lost or wounded men. The weeping began softly, building as each widowed woman's voice was added to the sound of sadness and death that filled the huge camp.

In the edge of the water, Willow held Water Bug, rocking and droning a sound that blended with all the others. Hers was not a loss in this camp, but a total loss of everyone in her family and village. The Sentu had not had anyone to weep for them. Here she mourned with the others and allowed herself to feel the loss as never before. Now perhaps her real healing could begin. She had closed her loss in a sealed box in her heart. Now the box had been forced open and pain gushed out.

Chief Dark Wolf stood in front of his tent. His right arm hung limp. An arrow had passed through the muscle and fallen in the dirt. His blood stained the ground as he shouted.

"Why?" But as he thought more about it, he felt he had at least part of the answer.

As the white men continued to grow in numbers, they pushed west. The villages that felt crowded soon found that the pioneers were invading their hunting grounds. The animals were fewer and more hunters sought them. Here at the summer council nearly every village represented had changed their location in the last few years. Perhaps the raiders didn't understand that they had been crowded out. Perhaps they thought that these people were deliberately taking their hunting ground. He understood that a good hunting territory was something worth fighting for, to maintain their claim.

"Moonflower, do not concern yourself. It is a simple wound that will heal. Please just cleanse and wrap it and then go see if you can help Sweet Grass with any of the others."

134

Two Feathers sought Willow and pulled Water Bug from the edge of the water. He held them both close for a moment.

"It is over," he said. "They are defeated. Soon Chief Dark Wolf will question the captives and then we will know what has caused them to come. You are safe now."

Willows tears continued to fall as she wandered the area carrying Water Bug. Many seemed to be nursing wounds or mourning the loss of someone from their village. I should do something but I don't know what to do, she thought. When she noticed Morning Dove, on her knees in the grass, she headed in that direction. Morning Dove was wrapping a chest wound in a young boy, too young to have been in the battle.

"He refused to go with his mother. He stayed to help defend the people," she said. Willow knelt and wiped the boy's face with a wet cloth.

"You were very brave," said Willow. "We thank you for protecting us. Would you like a drink of water?" She held the water dipper close to his lips so he could drink without lifting up.

The tears continued as the dead of the people were taken to the side of the camp and laid in the grass respectfully. The dead of the raiders were each tied over a horse and fastened together in a long string. They would be sent home with one of the captives.

After questioning the captives, Chief Dark Wolf had been told that they were in fact trying to force others from their hunting grounds. The Sentu had moved to the edge of it two years ago. One of their hunting parties had encountered a hunting party of the raiders and they had fought. The casualties had included their

Chief's eldest son. The Sentu, like others had only wanted to find a place to live that would grow their corn and provide meat without being confronted by the white men.

The shaman of the Omati took charge of preparing a large communal fire to send the spirits of the dead warriors to the spirit world. He sent word to the other holy men to come to his tent. He would hold a meeting with them to discuss what type of ceremony should be held since they had lost warriors from several different camps.

Chief Dark Wolf allowed the youngest captive warrior to leave camp, leading the horses with their dead. The other two men were secured to trees at the edge of camp and guarded. He sent a message to the Chief of the raiders.

"Come to talk. You will not be harmed. If you do not come after ten days, these men will be killed and their blood will be upon your head."

Chief Sky Fire did come, alone and clothed in such sadness that Chief Dark Wolf passed the peace pipe to him and they spent many hours talking with all the leaders at the summer council. They sympathized with his loss of his son, and even more so when they heard that his second son had been killed in the raid on the summer meeting.

Chief Sky Fire tried to explain.

"Many of my people starved during the past winter. We depend heavily on the buffalo, for food, clothing and warm tents, but the buffalo have not returned for many summers. I blamed the Sentu for the death of my first born, and then when the buffalo did not return to our hunting ground I felt it was their presence so close that caused the buffalo to go somewhere else. You no longer need to concern yourself with the Choyinaw, for we are few and weak. We have old women and children to feed, but our only hunters are old men or young mothers. We are lost. Allow me to take my two hunters and leave. You have nothing to fear from us ever again."

Chief Dark Wolf spoke.

"Chief Sky Fire is it true that you have only the three men left to hunt that we captured?"

"Yes, it is true."

"How many women and children are left behind?"

"There are twenty seven in all."

"Bring your people here. They can join the Blue Stone People. We always have plenty to eat and our men will hunt with yours. We have no desire to know that women and children are starving."

The other leaders nodded in agreement.

"The Choyinaw, are welcome here. You have faced a problem that was brought on by the white men. We will be strong together. Go now, take your hunters, and return with all your people as soon as possible."

Chief Sky Fire rose slowly and looked into the eyes of Chief Dark Wolf.

"If I ask you a question, will you answer it truthfully?"

"Yes, of course, I have no reason to lie to anyone."

"If I bring my wife and grandchild, and all the other women and children here, how do I know that you will not kill all that remains of my people?"

"We will not take revenge. Too many have died. Your people will live and grow strong again. Our common enemy is the white men. Return to your camp and tell your people that the People of the Blue Stone believe that we are all children of the Great Spirit. Your people have nothing to fear here. We will help you."

"You and these people are compassionate. Never have I been treated so kindly. I trust you. I will bring those who remain in our camp. They will be frightened to come, expecting retribution for the raid, but somehow I will convince them. Thank you, all of you. I will hurry."

His two hunters were released and they left camp together.

"Are you sure you are doing the right thing? His ways are vicious. You heard the report from the boy, Two Feathers, about the way they tortured his Chief."

"Yes, my friend, I am sure. He has lost nearly all his men. He will bring women and children and the old ones. If I am right, most of the widows will remarry here before the summer meeting is over. We have many young men here at the summer council. They will gain status by taking on the obligation of a family. If I allow such marriages, his people will be absorbed by the many camps that are here. I will insist that the old ones go with their families so no one camp is burdened more than it can handle. Chief Sky Fire can join our hunters and warriors. Growling Bear will keep him in check. We can all be sure of that."

"We must hold a communal fire and explain to the people why the raid happened and what we must do about it. It will be difficult for those who have lost a family member to accept the Choyinaw. We must encourage them to be kind and show their understanding. I wish that Sarah were here. She always knows what to say or do to sway the people in the right direction."

All the clans stayed longer than usual at the place of the summer council and by the time that they were gathering their belongings for the long trip home, only a few of the Choyinaw had chosen not to join other camps. Nine new people prepared to travel with the Blue Stone People and among those were Two Feathers, Willow and Water Bug.

They had left the main camp two days earlier knowing that they would need the time to harvest the corn they had planted at the little camp across the stream. Willow was amazed when they packed the horses at the many things they had accumulated during their stay there.

As the column of moving people passed them, they joined at chosen positions. Willow rode Lady and Water Bug was happy to be on Grandmother. She rode near Moonflower and Snow Star where she could visit as they traveled.

Two Feathers pulled the black stallion in line with the other young Blue Stone hunters, glad to be accepted as a valuable member of the camp. He led the rest of their horses on long lines. Each carried a load of packs and bundles. He planned to place their tent out of the main circle when they arrived. He wanted to keep his camp a bit separate. We are the people of The Lion, he thought. I don't want to blend in with the rest.

Two Feathers was deep in thought when his friend spoke to him.

"Two Feathers, what are you thinking about? I asked if you have ever been buffalo hunting."

"No, I haven't. I am looking forward to learning how it is done. When will the buffalo come?"

"They usually come when the snow gets deep farther north."

Two Feathers could not have imagined the many adventures that he would experience, living with the Blue Stone People but he couldn't help but measure his small band of three against the impressive people they had chosen to live near.

Two Feathers looked ahead at the column of people moving slowly across the grass of the prairie. He rode his black stallion beside Spotted Feather. He was from the Omati and Flying Eagle took him in to his tent and family two years earlier when he lost his father. He had no other family. I wonder if I will ever feel comfortable with these people. They hold their heads high and every one of them is wearing the blue stones that have become their symbol.

I can't see Willow from here. She pulled her horse up beside Snow Star, the Chief's daughter. I don't think Willow is aware that they are all traveling in positions assigned by status. They have been kind to us because of all that has happened but he may not approve of her assuming that it is alright to ride wherever she wants.

When the Chief invited us to stay in his tent during the entire summer council, I'm sure that gave us status with the people. Moonflower, his wife was good to us, too, and the others saw it.

Someday, Willow and I will lead our own people. It may not be so very far in the future. I wonder what Water Bug will be like when he is grown. He is such a fun little fellow. I know that he will always want to live near water. He loves it. He smiled.

"Spotted Feather, will you hold these leads for me? I will be right back. I am going to go see if Willow needs help.

It wasn't long after they arrived in camp that they were settled in a comfortable double walled tent situated to the left and a bit behind the communal tent.

As Two Feathers got to know the many hunters of the Blue Stone People, he realized that they had absorbed people from many other villages. Their prosperity at the trading spot had brought them favor with all the people at the summer meetings. Young people and some not so young, longed to be included in the prestige that the blue stones brought. He had met Flying Eagle and Spotted Feather. They were from the Omati. He soon learned that the craft of making beautiful jewelry with silver had come from their people. He had met Debon and heard about his village suffering the fate of his own. Now he had come face to face in battle with the Choyinaw, but even though they had taken credit for the raid on the Sentu, something didn't quite mesh. Willow had described the warriors that attacked their village. The raiders at the summer council didn't match her description and the arrow that he had kept and brought back to camp didn't look like those used by the Choyinaw. He knew there was deception here, but he wasn't sure who was telling lies or why.

He and Willow, and Water Bug lived near and under the protective eye of Chief Dark Wolf. For the sake of his family, he was glad that they did.

At first the Chief found it amusing that they had decided to take a new name and to try to become a new people, but with time as Two Feather's strength and confidence grew, he began to build an allegiance with other new comers and the younger men in camp. It seemed that his young age was insignificant when measured against his accomplishments. It wasn't long before two other young couples had moved their tents in line with his.

Debon had chosen Sheltah. She and Willow developed a close friendship. Debon felt his presence near Two Feathers brought him favor with the Blue Stone People.

Actually Chief Dark Wolf felt troubled by the new positioning of tents. He feared that the status of some of the older hunters and warriors was in some way being lessened.

CHAPTER TEN
WINTER COMES

The number of people in camp had increased. Father Bob was amazed when he saw the new faces and new tents going up in the camp of the Blue Stone People when they returned. They had been away far longer than he had expected.

After a couple of days of rest, Chief Dark Wolf called Bending Grass over to his tent. He told him to spread the word that tomorrow the women should prepare a feast for sundown. The Chief chuckled to himself. That young man likes to talk. He will have the job done in no time, he thought

He saw Growling Bear and asked him to take six of his seasoned hunters and to hunt for fresh meat enough for the entire camp to have at the feast.

"That may take more than one night," he replied.

"It better not. I am also sending the new young hunters out with the same instructions. I thought I should let you know that Night Hawk said he saw dust on the prairie this morning, far west of here. If it is buffalo, you will be able to down enough to feed this camp all winter. Just send a rider back to get the women. We will postpone the feast if it is buffalo. I will send the young hunters east to the long grass. The rest of the men will be needed here to stand guard in the usual places. You should assign the positions and the men to change shifts before you leave."

"Yes, my Chief." Growling Bear mounted his horse and within a few minutes, Chief Dark Wolf saw new guards in position. Chief Dark Wolf walked to the tent of Two Feathers.

"Two Feathers are you in there?"

"Yes, my Chief," he said as he stepped out.

"I would have you lead a hunting party to the east toward the tall grass. You may take six hunters with you. I need the rest of the men here to guard our camp. It would be good to have fresh meat in camp for the feast the women are planning for tomorrow night. Go quickly and choose men that you know will hunt wisely."

"Yes, my Chief. I am honored."

As Chief Dark Wolf walked back to the center of camp, he could see Two Feathers scrambling to gather a hunting party. It surprised him to see that Two Feathers had Hondor and Kier with him as well as Snapping Turtle and three others. It is interesting that he didn't choose his young peers but more seasoned hunters. I'm impressed. Perhaps he is wiser than I thought.

Soon after that, Growling Bear, Flying Eagle and five others left camp, through the big rocks.

Night Hawk rode into camp and reported that the hunting parties had gone in opposite directions.

"Thank you Night Hawk. I can always count on you to be watchful. Please return to your position outside of the big rocks. I appreciate your message. It is valuable to me."

Chief Dark Wolf automatically moved to the little knoll and sat down to view the camp below him. Father Bob joined him with a big smile. It was the first opportunity that he had felt comfortable approaching the Chief since his return. He wondered if all the new people, bringing new beliefs would weaken the immature faith of the people. He cautiously opened the subject, hoping not to offend.

"Chief Dark Wolf, my friend, it is good to see you and your growing camp back from your travels and looking well. I have detected many new faces."

"Yes much has happened and most of them have had to face evil as strong as you did. They probably don't recognize it as such, but it is true. The remnants of three villages have joined us in the past year. The Great Spirit has spared these few from destruction."

"Then it is our job to teach them that they were spared to honor Him. Was it the soldiers?"

"No. In each case, it was camps moving to find a hunting ground, as the white men come, more and more. The camps war over territory and soon a whole people is lost. The Soldiers have raided many camps, but the people that have joined us have lost everything in wars with other villages. It is sad. When I was a boy, we did not hear of such things."

"New people bring different ways of doing things and new beliefs. I hope that the Blue Stone People are strong enough to be teachers of the right way," said Father Bob. "One of the youngsters said that you are planning a feast tomorrow evening. May I come?"

"Father Bob, our people respect you and would miss you if you did not. You are always welcome in our camp and the big tent. You are stronger than any of us and we haven't forgotten that you fought that evil thing and that the Great Spirit was on your side. Please come, even if you can't sing," he said laughing. They laughed together and then Father Bob stood and returned to the church. He could feel a new, source of opposition in the camp. He needed to pray.

Chief Dark Wolf studied the activity in camp, detecting certain people staying back and keeping themselves separate. Sleeping Bear had been slightly wounded in the raid on the summer meeting but it hadn't stopped him from taking in an old woman from the Choyinaw that had no family. He was proud of him and Dancing Willow. It is not so hard now, but winter will make it difficult to have a new person in their family. He wondered what he could do to make it more comfortable. He watched as Blue Stone brought her little girl, Happy Song over to talk to the old woman. They were smiling.

I think it is time that Sleeping Bear receives his old name back and his status as my second warrior and hunter. Flying Eagle won't like it, but he must still learn that respect is earned and doesn't come by marrying my daughter. He is lacking in compassion, too. He objected when he heard that the Choyinaw were all coming to the summer meeting to join new people. He still thinks that his work at the trading spot makes him equal to Growling Bear. It doesn't, at least not in my eyes.

As he stood he was surprised to have Flying Eagle ride swiftly up to him. He felt embarrassed at his thoughts and was glad that the excited young man in front of him couldn't read his thoughts.

"Chief Dark Wolf, they come. Many buffalo are coming! The hunters you sent east saw the dust and have joined us. We are all waiting until they get nearer." He turned his horse and rode away without giving the Chief time to say anything.

The Chief told Moonflower that she would not be going this time.

146

"You are needed here, and I don't think you should work so hard. There are many women here that are capable workers. Choose who will go among the women. Make sure they take everything they will need." When he told her where the herd was, she groaned.

"There is no water source where they are traveling. If they let the herd come close enough, they could bring the meat here to process it by the lake."

"That has never been done before, but it would work if the herd comes near the big rocks," he agreed.

"Can't your men make sure they do?"

"Yes if our hunters are careful and patient. I will go make sure they understand what we need them to do. Have some of the experienced women come to help prepare the animals for the short trip through the rocks. The men here should be able to make some travois that will fit through the path in the rocks. I'll assign that job before I leave."

He swung up on his horse and moved away and she immediately sent several women scurrying to announce a meeting for all the women in the big tent, right away. By the time she had a pan of water on and tea heating; the tent was filling with women. Some of them had never been in a tent as large as that one. She started to talk before they were all settled.

"Our hunters are bringing a herd of buffalo near the big rocks. They will execute the hunt there. Chief Dark Wolf has asked that women with experience to be ready to prepare the animals to bring back to camp. I believe that we should send at least ten. The rest of us will gather our drying racks near the lake and then make lots more. With help from the Great Spirit, we will have plenty of good, rich buffalo meat this winter."

As if that was his cue, Father Bob stepped into the big tent.

"Hello ladies. I am Father Bob. Most of you know me, but I see a few new faces here. I heard that the hunters have found buffalo. Let's pray for the safety of our hunters and true aim for their shots. Please raise your hands. Holy Father, Creator of heaven and earth, we thank you for the bounty of your provision for the people. We ask your blessing on the hunters and hunted that no one is injured and that the animals that give their lives for our food will not suffer. Thank you for bringing the animals to our hunting grounds so that we may have a winter of plenty. Amen"

"Amen," said most of the women.

"I am going to leave right away. I hope that Chief Dark Wolf will allow me to take one buffalo to fill the cache in the church." He hurried away and soon rode out on one of the horses that had been Father Pete's leading two of his pack mules.

Okallah and Gamier volunteered as soon as Father Pete stepped out.

"We will go. We have both been at a buffalo hunt and know what we must do."

"Please Moonflower, will you allow me to go? I have never seen a buffalo. I would like to see the herd before it is disturbed by the hunters. I promise I will work hard. The others can show me what to do," said Butterfly.

"Yes, if it means that much to you. I need more that are willing to go. Who else will go?"

Others stood and said they would go get their things and pack a horse. Those that are going should meet back here as soon as you are ready. Be sure to take a good sharp knife," she reminded them, "and extra pack horses."

Falling Stones and Gray Cloud approached Moonflower They offered to carry any available drying racks to the high ground beside the church.

"I think that we will work on this side of the lake. We shouldn't work with all that blood by the church."

"That's fine. Just tell us where you want them. She pointed and he nodded. After we gather them there, do you want us to cut new branches for more racks?"

"Yes, Falling Stones that would be a big help. Thank you." He is such a kindhearted man, she thought. She didn't need to know that Chief Dark Wolf had given him orders to see that they helped the women in any way they could. He was always helpful.

*****

As the women quietly approached their hunters, they could see the animals clearly. The very small herd was moving slowly and coming closer to the big rocks with every step. Butterfly was so excited that Gamier placed her hand over Butterfly's mouth. She softly whispered in her ear.

"Any sound can send them running away. Be very still."

When Growling Bear finally gave the signal to choose an animal and shoot, the massive beasts were so near that the women felt afraid. They stared as one after another grunted and peacefully dropped to the ground. Each arrow hit its mark with precision. Two Feathers waited until Hondor pointed out a young, fat

149

bull for him. He pulled his bow back to its max and dropped the bull with excellent skill just as the herd began to run. Hondor praised his ability and strength.

"You are a very good bowman, Two Feathers. I wish Debon had come with us. He has not hunted buffalo. He will be unhappy that he missed this opportunity."

"Yes, it is my error. I should have asked him to come. I see that Kier has taken a large cow. She will feed many." It was not until that moment that Hondor lifted his rifle and dropped two buffalo as they ran past. He had not shot sooner, knowing that the sound would start them running. The other hunters had all used bows. Growling Bear nodded approval at each hunter, grinning broadly.

Chief Dark Wolf was smiling as the meat was moved to camp. Father Bob had shot after Hondor. He was distressed that he had not killed the animal he had shot. He took one of the empty travois and followed the trail and dust made by the running herd. It wasn't long before he saw the young cow still trying to run, but lagging far behind the others. He shot again and had the meat he needed for winter, but it was a cheerless victory. He was glad that the other hunters could not see him as tears slid down his face. He felt wretched knowing that the young cow had suffered at his hand.

Somehow I must improve my shooting skill. He was far behind the others as he came through the opening in the big rocks. He had returned slowly, sensing that the small herd might be the last herd of buffalo that he ever got to hunt. Coyote and Gray Cloud still cheered for him and then helped him unload the heavy animal near his outdoor fire pit. He had many drying racks that he had made. He brought them from behind the church. He couldn't help but smile when he thought about the first time that Father Pete had tried to help preserve meat.

He didn't have to work alone. Two women came with their sharp knives and helped until all his meat was sliced thin and hanging on the racks. Thank you, Spotted Fawn and Butterfly. You have been kind to help me. He made a mental note to take each of them a small surprise when he could.

"Thank you, good job. God bless you," he said. It had become a tradition to say it anytime someone worked with him. They laughed and said it back. Most of the people in camp spoke some English now and it made it a lot easier for him to tell stories and to teach.

Fires burned brightly near the lake as many women worked through the night getting all the fresh meat sliced and on the racks. The hides would bring warmth as robes or strong additional space in tents after they were worked.

*****

"Moonflower, I have been thinking a lot about Sleeping Bear and Dancing Willow. He couldn't hunt because of his wounded shoulder. I would like to do something that is long overdue. I am thinking of giving him back his second hunter status and putting his tent next to Growling Bear's. Also I want to give him back his old name. It was a selfless act of kindness taking in the old woman from the Choyinaw. They have given her a new family. I don't remember her name. Do you?"

"Yes, her name is Smiling Moon. She is sweet and will be a second Grandmother for Happy Song. Blue Stone said the baby likes her already."

151

"What do you think about giving Sleeping Bear back his status?"

"Oh, I don't know about these things. You usually don't discuss such things with me. Why are you asking now?"

"Moonflower, I am asking because I am wondering how it will affect our daughter. If I make Sleeping Bear second hunter it will surely anger Flying Eagle."

"Now that you say that, I think it is cause for thought. You could call a meeting of a select few and include Flying Eagle. Just discuss it with all of them about giving Sleeping Bear back his old name."

"Thank you Moonflower that is good advice." He hugged her gently. "I think that is what I will do."

As the day sped by, the women that had worked so hard preparing the meat for drying, rested. Others watched the meat and kept the fires burning. The camp was relatively quiet.

The following morning Chief Dark Wolf held his small meeting in the big tent. It was brief and all the men agreed that Sleeping Bear should be given his old name back.

"When do you plan on doing it?" Flying Eagle asked with a somber face.

"I think we should do it as soon as the women can fix us a good feast," answered Chief Dark Wolf. "I am looking forward to tasting some of that buffalo meat."

Growling Bear held back and when the rest of the men had left, he asked the question that Chief Dark Wolf was concerned about answering.

"My Chief, if you give back his old name, you will also give back his status. That would upset Flying Eagle. He and I are not the best of friends but I am sure that he thinks of himself as second hunter. He might move back to the Omati if he gets offended enough. You would be sorrowful to not see Watching Owl grow up. Snow Star and Moonflower would be separated. She has lost two daughters. You may cause her to lose a third. I say this as a friend, my Chief. Flying Eagle has been a Father to Spotted Feather. He took him in as Sleeping Bear has taken the old woman. Would a reward for such responsibility be appropriate? It would salve his feelings and be an example of approval for others."

"Thank you Growling Bear, your thoughts are helpful. I must think on all of this. I am going for a walk."

He strolled slowly through camp, nodding to Sky Fire and his wife, Rippling Water. His tent and that of their last and youngest son, Young Blood, and his wife, Meadow Lark and their daughter, Rain Drop, sat in a small clearing at the back of the lake, too close to the spot where the guard stood to keep people from entering the woods near the trail along the bluff. Sky Fire is another one that wants to have the security of the large camp but he hopes to stay separate, to retain his title as Chief. These are troubling times. I may have to hold another meeting with the new people. I don't want our camp building divisions. He stopped to talk to the shepherds.

"The sheep look healthy and with your good care they have added to their number. Is there anything that is needed for you or the sheep before winter?"

"Chief Dark Wolf, would you please choose other young men to learn the sheep song and to care for them? We have watched over the sheep since the day that Singing Wind and Sharp Knife brought them here. Although it is an honor that you think us worthy of the responsibility, it is our desire to be included in the activities of the other young men in our camp. We would like to hunt and ride the prairie learning new skills like tracking and scouting. We were not included in the buffalo hunt. We were not even told what was happening until it was all over."

"I will think on it. You are both doing a very good job. Not everyone could do so well," he said with a broad smile."

He walked to his knoll, hoping that no one would disturb him. He had many issues to think about and decisions to make.

*****

It took several men's help and four women to get the buffalo calf into the huge pit that radiated intense heat from the glowing coals in the bottom. As the loose cover was put on, the women gave a sigh of relief.

"I don't know what that metal rack was used for by the white men, but it works well to hold that calf off the coals," said Rippling Water. "Is there anything else that I can help with before I go back? Sky Fire, always likes me to stay where he can see me. That way he can yell if he wants something."

"Now that we have the meat cooking, we can start any other food that we want to share. I have many cooking stones heating at my cooking fire. I am going to make stacks of corn cakes," said Morning Dove.

"That's nice, I don't know what to make."

"Walk back to my tent with me. We can think of something."

Moonflower watched as the two women crossed the center of camp. She took a big clay pot and walked to the side of the lake near the church to get fresh water. It will be a long time before the lake water seems clean again to me. I don't like the thought of all that blood near our water supply.

She glanced up in the direction of the horse herd. Well, we didn't get very far with building that fence. I wonder if it is too late to do it now. It hasn't been mentioned since Father Pete died. That was a sad thing. It has been a whole year. It doesn't seem possible. I wonder if another priest will come one day.

She walked slowly back to her tent, balancing the water jar on her shoulder.

CHAPTER ELEVEN
A NEW WAY OF LIVING

As the people gathered at the big communal fire, Chief Dark Wolf noticed the Blue Stone People sitting in their usual places, while the new arrivals looked for places to indicate their imagined status.

He stood, asking everyone else to stand. When they had, he asked for every young hunter with a wife and only one child to come and stand with his family, behind Moonflower. Some were laughing while others looked puzzled.

"Now, would any young man that has a wife but no children, come stand in front of them?" The others moved back as the young couples stepped in front of them.

"Next, any young hunters that have taken their three day journey, but have not yet taken a wife, come and stand in front of them. That is good, the rest of my hunters that have two or more children come stand across from me, with your families.

Now hear me well my people." He paused for a long time, looking at the groups clustered together. "The people you stand near share your status. No one is higher or lower. Some are younger and have much energy. Others are older and have experience and wisdom. This is what I would have you do. All those who are parents but your children are grown, come stand beside me. He paused to give them time to get up off their blankets and walk to the area he had indicated. In this group we have a man that has taken on new responsibilities. He has added to his family, a grandmother. Her name is Smiling Moon. We welcome

156

her." Everyone applauded and cheered. The people of the Choyinaw cheered the loudest. For his bravery as a warrior and his skill as a hunter, we honor him: but more for his being a responsible head of a growing household, we honor Standing Bear!"

The man was caught totally off guard. Dancing Willow began to wipe away tears of joy.

"My seasoned hunters, all of them, with raised children, will move their tents, in a row behind the big tent. Growling Bear is number one hunter and warrior. No one else is above or below anyone else. His tent will stand in the middle of the row. When I need my wise men, for a meeting, they will be close at hand, not scattered all over camp. The families with more than one child will join that line, some to the left and some behind those. Families with one child will set their tents to the right of my councilmen. All the rest of the young men, not yet married will move their tents to the path that goes to the corn field. The ground beneath the tents will be built up as the big tent is, to help keep the floor dry. Those young hunters that are living with others are to make tents of your own. There is another one among the young families with one child that we should honor. Like his Blue Stone brother, he took on the responsibility of adding to his family. We are happy that he has brought Spotted Feather from the Omati. Flying Eagle we honor you. Your tent will be the first on the right of the council." The people continued to stand and applaud. "Now be sure that each of you digs a new cache for some of the wonderful buffalo meat we all smell." The people applauded again. "I have one final request. Any young man, not yet married, once you all have your tents in place come and tell me. I will have a meeting with all of you. I know that you all join me in welcoming the new members to the camp of the Blue Stone People. Now, I think we should each get some food and sit down with our new neighbors."

Moonflower leaned her head close to Chief Dark Wolf's ear.

"Aren't you the clever one? You breezed right past that status thing. This camp is going to be in total chaos until people get their tents set up in their new locations. I like what you did. It puts all the women of my age closer. Most of them will be behind the big tent. I think Sweet Water and Father Bob are the only two that aren't moving."

"Moonflower, you forgot us. We aren't moving either."

"You said you are planning a meeting for all the young hunters. What is that about?"

"I am going to have them all learn the song of the sheep and take turns caring for them. Also, I want to have one that is a message runner and when it is his turn, he can stay in the big tent so that he is near so he can be conveniently summoned."

"You have been doing a lot of planning. I am proud of you Dark Wolf. This will be a good thing. Now, everyone is waiting for us, we should go get some food."

People were milling around the food tables, ready to begin the feast. Father Bob stepped to the first table where platters of steaming meat were waiting to be sampled. He raised his hands and waited. It grew quiet. All that could be heard was the crackling of the big fire and a murmur from one of the new women.

"Heavenly Father, we thank you for our Chief and the wisdom that you have given him. We are excited to make the changes that he requires of us. Thank you for the new people that you have brought to our camp. They add strength, wisdom and new vitality. We will enjoy getting to know them, and thank you for all this delicious food. It looks and smells wonderful. Amen"

"Amen," the people said.

As the feasting began, Chief Dark Wolf listened carefully to hear any remarks, concerning the changes he announced.

Sky Fire came over to him and said that he thought it wouldn't work. "Warriors should be nearest the herd," he declared, as if he was the final word on the subject.

Chief Dark Wolf smiled agreeably and told him that since he had not been in this camp very long, that he probably had not noticed that the most seasoned warriors keep their favorite horse ready at the back of their tents at all times.

"You will probably want to do that, too. I noticed that Young Blood keeps his favorite horse near his tent."

"Are you suggesting that I am just a warrior now?"

"I am suggesting that good things are worth copying." He walked over to Sleeping Bear, now restored as Standing Bear, and asked him if he was glad to have his name returned to him.

"I think it means a lot to Dancing Willow. I had gotten used to Sleeping Bear. It didn't bother me that much anymore. After all this time, it will take some getting used to."

"Unsympathetic, I say. He doesn't care about the new ones at all." Rippling Water lowered her voice when she realized that others were hearing her.

"Mother we will be near you and near the big tent too. I think it is a good plan. You will see. I think he does care or he wouldn't have allowed us to come back with them."

"He could have at least explained why he was making everyone move. We just got set up. Now we have to take it down and move everything."

"It will be alright Mother. We will all help you."

*****

The people worked diligently, sharing tools and helping each other wherever it was needed. There weren't enough shovels in camp, to satisfy everyone. It took several days for all the tents to appear in the locations he had directed. He was amused at the way some of the young men had solved their problem of not having their own tent. They had combined to form a bachelor cooperative. Using their hides to make two unlined tents, and they planned to make more as hides became available. They tolerated their poor quarters while bargaining with the women to sew for them and they would pay with meat. They requested to be allowed to go hunting, but the Chief refused.

"There are many unused hides in this camp. You must figure out a way to earn them and have them made into tents." It took several weeks, before each of the young men had their own tent, with a cache in it, standing on the path to the corn field.

Two Feathers approached the Chief.

"Chief Dark Wolf, was it your intention to move my family when you said that the unmarried young men

160

should live way over there?" he pointed in the general direction.

"Yes. Is there a reason that you should be treated differently?" His humorless expression shut the door on any discussion. "You and Willow will be fine there. Have you dug a cache and lined it?"

"Yes and our tent is lined and packed with grass."

"Did you receive a three person share of the buffalo meat?"

"Yes, my Chief and we have wild grain and corn as well as some nuts."

"That is good. Tell the other young men that a meeting will be held in the big tent in the morning. I expect all of you there at sunrise." Two Feathers walked away scowling.

Night Hawk smiled and greeted the Chief.

"I was wondering if you had assigned anyone to watch the sheep, during the meeting. I will be glad to do it, if you want me to."

"Night Hawk, do you ever stop smiling?"

"Sometimes I think I do, when I am sleeping," he laughed. "Spotted Fawn will wake me in time to send the boys to your meeting."

"Thank you my friend. Come visit after the meeting. We will talk."

In the morning, Moonflower had a big pan of mint and lemon grass tea heating. She had sweetened it with honey and she had prepared a meat filling for the young men to eat, rolled in the remaining corn cakes.

"Please relax and have some tea and food while we talk," said Chief Dark Wolf as soon as all the young men had come in.

"First, I want to acknowledge White Grass and Pine Berry for the outstanding job that they have done with our sheep. They have endured bad weather and sung with sore throats. The sheep have remained healthy and happy and have multiplied. It is necessary for all of you to be able to guard our people and the animals we have, therefore I want you to remain here after our meeting is over and sing the sheep song until you all know it. Sing it just as they do. From now on you ten men are going to become our night guard. Step out of the tent with me for a moment and I will show you where the positions are that you will guard."

In the dirt outside the big tent he drew with a stick, outlining the camp and placed dots for the tents and a circle for the lake. He put dots for every location that had tents including the big tent. He marked it with an X.

"This is our camp," he said. "There is the church, the horse herd and the sheep hill. Over there begins the big rocks and all this is woods and finally the prairie. We have nine locations that require an alert man on guard." He poked the dirt in each of the locations. Study the map until you have it memorized. Count with me the spots to guard." He pointed at each in turn, over and over until finally he asked Pine Berry to count them in order. He did it correctly.

"Two Feathers, you do it next." He did it correctly. "Good, I hope that if I ask you, each of you can tell me where position five is." They all pointed to the prairie side of the big rocks. "That is correct. Cat Claw, go get ash from the fire and circle this drawing. No one is to walk on it. Two Feathers, you are to guard position number one. If I ride my horse at night and check the guard positions, where will you be?"

"I will be just inside the trees on the back side of the lake."

He assigned numbers to the ten young men.

"I will be on the other side of the woods beyond the spring."

"I will be at the start of the path by the big rocks."

Each responded appropriately. "Spots eight and nine, are to guard the sheep." He deliberately assigned Pine Berry again to the sheep, as number eight, but number nine was Cat Claw. "The tenth man is White Grass. He will stay in the big tent at night and be a ready messenger for me to summon. At the start of the new moon, we will have another meeting at sunrise. Remember it and be here, I will not want to have to remind you. You are guards. I expect you to be responsible." It was his intention to change their numbers at each meeting. He stood and said he was leaving. "What are you going to do?"

"We are staying to learn to sing the sheep song," they all answered. He nodded and walked out, but was followed by Pine Berry.

"I was hoping that you would give me any assignment but the sheep," he said it in a whiney voice.

"You will be there as long as it pleases me, or until you have trained Cat Claw so that the sheep will follow him anywhere he walks!"

"I understand now, thank you my Chief," he said with a grin. "I'm going in and teach them the sheep song now," he said gladly.

"Good, tell White Grass that I need him."

"White Grass, you will be my messenger. First tell the night guard that they stand guard from sundown until they are relieved at first light. Then go tell everyone at each tent that they are not to walk on this drawing."

"Yes, my Chief." He hurried away.

Chief Dark Wolf held similar meetings with the different groups. He was tired of assigning positions, but by the end of the second day, every man in camp knew what his responsibilities were and when they were to be performed. He had a crew of craftsmen that would work with Flying Eagle to mine the turquoise and some were assigned to go with him to the trading spot. Their families would also be going.

Father Bob had watched the frenzied activity as the people worked to prepare the new locations for their tents and he thought it peculiar until a few days later he could make sense of it all. The changed layout of the camp made perfect sense to him. Young mothers were together. Old ladies that knew weaving and sewing lived near each other. Those with grown families were the teachers or advisors. It all worked. The hunters were grouped together and near the big tent. Those same men were the warriors that could now be easily alerted. This didn't just happen, it took a lot of planning, he thought.

When he saw Chief Dark Wolf sitting on his knoll, Father Bob eagerly joined him. He volunteered his total approval.

"I appreciate your saying that. I had to figure out a way to match the new people up with others in similar circumstances. Sky Fire wants to retain his Chief status, and Two Feathers wants to live here while building a new people. It is difficult to satisfy everyone, but I'm hoping this will work at least for a while."

"Change is never easy for some people," said Father Bob. "I am worrying what strange new beliefs they have brought. Would you come over and eat with me and then stay for evening Mass. It is lonely over there since I lost Father Pete."

"Yes, I will come, but first I need to go let Moonflower know that she doesn't have to worry about feeding me tonight."

"It would be nice to have her come, too. Bring her with you," he said as he left the knoll.

I think I will surprise him with a few more guests. Maybe we can find out just what they do believe in.

The Chief walked slowly across the center of camp and noticed the pattern of many footprints going around his drawing. He strolled behind the big tent and scratched at the door of Sky Fire and Rippling Water.

"You may come."

"I greet you both and bring an invitation from our priest, Father Bob. He wishes us to visit and eat with him.

Rippling Water was pleased and said so.

"No one else in this camp has offered us as much as a drink of water. My husband is Chief of the Choyinaw and should be treated with more respect!"

"Woman, hold your tongue."

"Has someone said something to you that was offensive?" asked Chief Dark Wolf.

"No she is upset because our tent is here with others. We are used to being separate and distinctive."

"I think what you are saying is that you were the privileged. Sky Fire, I understand but there is only one Chief in this camp and that is me. I have placed you in the center of my seasoned councilors. I will need your superior wisdom in the times ahead. Please come to my tent soon, and we will walk to the church together."

He stepped out quickly, motioning for White Grass.

"Take this message to the priest. Tell him that Moonflower and I are bringing Sky Fire and Rippling Water to visit."

"Yes my Chief," replied White Grass and he took off at a fast run.

Chief Dark Wolf stepped in his tent to see Moonflower pulling on a new shirt that she had just finished embellishing, with swirls of tiny beads and carefully cut fringe at the bottom.

"You look lovely, Moonflower. I am always proud to walk with you through our camp. Your new shirt is beautiful. I haven't seen it before."

"I just finished it."

"I like it. Do you have some food made that we can take to Father Bob's? He has asked us to come to visit and eat with him, and I have asked Sky Fire and Rippling Water to join us. They will be here soon.

"Well I have this buffalo stew and I can quickly make some crackers."

"That will be fine." She hurried to get the batter made for the crackers, and lined a basket with a piece of bright yellow cloth. In the center she placed a small pot of honey and as the crackers were taken from the cooking stone, she placed them artistically around the pot.

"There, we can take those and he will probably have a few left for his breakfast."

"Thank you Moonflower."

Sky Fire and Rippling Water, had changed their clothes and looked every bit unique and individual.

Chief Dark Wolf smiled his best smile and hoped that the visit would go well.

Father Bob had done an efficient job of setting up a comfortable place in the corner of the church for them all to sit and eat. He had a very small fire going in the center with a pan of tea steaming nearby.

When they arrived bringing a large pot of buffalo stew, with garden vegetables from the trading spot, his delight was genuine. Rippling Water nodded and handed him a loosely corked crock of a fermented drink. He could tell it was potent by its odor.

"Thank you, thank you very much. Welcome to the church and my home, too he said laughing. One day I hope to build a small house nearby but for now, this is all the comforts that I can offer you," he said apologetically. "I am Father Bob."

"This is Sky Fire, my valued council advisor, and his wife, Rippling Water," said Chief Dark Wolf. "Moonflower is my wife," he said for the benefit of the new people.

"We have met. Moonflower has been very helpful," said Rippling Water.

"This drink that you brought, is it to be served before our meal or after?" Father Bob sniffed it again and left the cork out.

"In our camp it was served often and plentifully. I am sorry that we have so little left," said Sky Fire. "Next summer I will show you how to make it, when the fruit is available."

Father Bob brought five coffee cups and put a tiny splash in the bottom of each. He handed the first to Chief Dark Wolf, and then one to Sky Fire, one to each of the women and the last was for himself. Sky Fire held his cup out to the group and so the rest did the same, waiting.

"We drink together, to forget the pain of loss. We drink to fade the fear and memories and we drink to warm our hearts and celebrate a new way of living." He spoke slowly and softly. Quickly he downed the small portion and held his cup for a refill. Father Bob had found the drink very sweet and very strong. It burned his tongue, throat and now was heating his stomach. Firmly he planted the cork back in the bottle.

"I have the perfect tea to follow that," he said, dipping his gourd ladle and pouring tea into all the cups. Moonflower's face was red and she looked like she had been poisoned. He had been made uncomfortable by the drink, too. He served the food with Moonflower's help and Rippling Water made sure that Sky Fire was given a more than ample portion. I think she is having a worse time adjusting than her husband, thought Father Bob as he observed.

"Tell us about some of the customs and traditions of your people. I will be holding a Christian ceremony here after we have visited and I hope that you will enjoy staying and experiencing the Holy Mass with Chief Dark Wolf and Moonflower."

"The Choyinaw took part in many rituals. The warriors were strong and skilled. They would pit their strength against each other in order to become even stronger. They were rewarded for the spoils of war by receiving slaves or other things of value. Our shaman, Night Crier, held ceremonies for the spirits. He had an altar where he poured the blood of animals and prayed. The more he prayed, the more our enemies were weakened. This ceremony you will hold tonight, is it a blood ceremony?"

"Yes in a way it is, but quite different from the one you are used to seeing. We do not kill animals for spiritual ceremonies, only when it is necessary for food, like the buffalo in this stew. One man was killed long ago. He was the Son of God. His name was Jesus. He died so that no one else would have to die. His death is depicted on the cross outside."

Moonflower felt the conversation had become far too heavy and she tried to lighten the mood by commenting on the patterns that decorated the clothing of Sky Fire and Rippling Water.

"Did you do the bead work on your dress and Sky Fire's shirt? The colors are pretty. The patterns are very different."

"I make all our clothes. The patterns are the story of our lives."

"That is fascinating. What do you mean? How can you tell a story with beads?"

"The first row has five white beads. Each bead represents a child. The yellow bead under the white bead shows that my third child was a girl. The red beads under the white and yellow, tells that they are dead," she said showing no emotion. You can see that I have one son that lives. He is here with us."

"I am so sorry that you have lost four children. I lost one, a girl. Then Dark Wolf brought me a girl, but she is grown now and has gone back to her white family. She visits occasionally. Her name is Sarah. I have one daughter left that lives here. She is Snow Star. She is married to Flying Eagle and they have a son named Watching Owl. Their tent is not far from yours."

"Why did you let your slave go?"

"She was not a slave. I raised her as a daughter. She became a healer and she is the one that taught us all about the Great Spirit and His Son Jesus."

"So your daughter was a shaman." Sky Fire stated it rather than asking.

"No she is a Christian," said Father Bob, breaking into the conversation before it could get off track. Sarah has an amazing, strong faith in the One True God."

"Rippling Water, you were telling us about the meaning of the patterns on your clothes."

"Some other time perhaps, but now I am tired." She stood abruptly and even Sky Fire was caught off guard. She stretched across the distance and took the crock of fermented drink, carefully wrapping her arm around it. He rose and nodded to those still seated and just like that they were out the door and gone.

"Did I say something wrong?" puzzled Father Bob.

"No but I think she was not willing to tell us the meaning for the other strange symbols," said Moonflower.

"Chief Dark Wolf, what did you think of his strong drink?"

"I think it is not something that I want my hunters to start making and drinking. If we had served them more of that, they might have stayed a little longer. We did learn quite a bit about them though."

Father Bob prepared for mass. Chief Dark Wolf wondered why he wore black vestments.

"Our new people have lost so many loved ones, family and friends. We need the mass for the dead, but we must also pray for those here, burdened with pain. Their very lifestyle conceived misery."

170

CHAPTER TWELVE
STIRRING THE POT

The Abalinah had been creative; fabricating much of the history they had related. They sought sympathy and wanted to appear as victims. They had heard of the successful Blue Stone People and secretly scoffed at their peaceful ways. The competitive behavior of their women at the games had to be explained away as trying too hard to feel worthy of being accepted and the humble demeanor of Hondor, Kier, and Debon was to create a non-combative acceptance by the men of the Blue Stone People.

They quickly figured out that Growling Bear and Flying Eagle were the two men with which they needed to garner favor. Chief Dark Wolf was a strong leader, but his acceptance had been easily obtained by simply being there. Day by day they lived with the people and worked at blending in and not causing any confrontations.

Now with the people feeling the upheaval of the new camp layout and the distraction of still more new people in the village, Hondor relaxed. He had an awareness of the friction that always lay under the surface, when Growling Bear and Flying Eagle were near each other. He thought that he could use that to his advantage. He simply had to figure out how.

It had been a year, since they had joined the Blue Stone People. Neither he nor the others had been allowed to see where the blue stones were collected. It was obvious by the way that the woods behind the lake was guarded that the source had to be somewhere in

171

the woods between the lake and the prairie beyond. He hoped that his patience would eventually pay off.

As he pulled one of his horses from the herd, he watched Gray Cloud mounting one of the young mares and riding her in the lake. Back and forth they went. She whirled and bucked but he managed to stay on. He was laughing as he slid off.

"Hi Hondor, did you want to take a turn? She bites and she will drop you in the water if she gets a chance."

"No I thought I would take a ride in the north woods and see if any of our horses wandering off in that direction. My big gray is missing from the herd. You know we started to make a fence. Whatever happened to that idea?" He asked as he placed a soft bit on his horse and slid up with no saddle.

"You better take a rope if you are going to bring any horses back," said Gray Cloud, offering his with an extended arm.

"Thanks he said, but didn't take it. "I just want to get out of camp for a while. If I see any horses I will head them back this way." Then contrary to what he had said, he headed through the big rocks.

That was peculiar, thought Gray Cloud. He didn't even take a bow or gun.

With the guards in place, Hondor couldn't enter the woods from the prairie side, but he noticed that there were two within fifty big paces from the end of the bluff. He rode slowly over to Spotted Feather and asked if he was as bored as he looked.

"I'm glad that it is quiet. That means the people in the village are safe. Snow Star, Flying Eagle and Watching Owl are my family now, I don't mind taking a turn to guard them."

"Are you sure that's what you are guarding, or is it his precious blue stones?"

"Both," he answered without thinking. "Well I mean they are both worth guarding."

"Yes, they are," said Hondor with a grin. He rode back to camp the way he had come and tied the horse beside his tent, telling Okallah to water it and rub it down. She did, but not with the kind touch of appreciation. She resented some of the tasks that she had been required to do since coming to live with the Blue Stone People. This isn't how I thought it would be at all. Everything is taking too long.

*****

"I agree that we have not had fun at the summer meetings for a couple years. First we had the earthquake and couldn't go and then last year the raid and we were waiting for the Choyinaw to return and choose a people to follow. We only ended up with six of them and only one is a hunter. Young Blood would take part, too. We could all use some fun. The games at the Summer Meeting weren't that much fun this year, because of the raid and people were upset."

"I don't know Gray Cloud, let's talk to Growling Bear. He is the one that was eager to do it, but he hasn't mentioned it since Father Pete died. No one has."

"Cat Claw, would you ask Growling Bear to come to my tent. He doesn't need to hurry. I just want to ask him something."

"Yes my Chief."

In just a few minutes Growling Bear and Cat Claw returned together. The young messenger sat down on one of the logs that circled the ashes of the communal fire pit. He would patiently wait in the area until he would be needed again.

Growling Bear and the Chief sat down outside the Chief's tent and Moonflower brought two cups of tea and a tray covered with tasty morsels of dried meat, berries and shelled nuts. On the side of the tray she had placed a row of crackers and crunchy greens.

"Will you need anything else? I want to go talk to Rippling Water."

"No this is more than we needed," answered Dark Wolf with a smile. "You don't have to hurry back. We are fine."

Growling Bear chuckled at her as she hurried away.

"Big Flower is the same. She wants to feed me all the time." He scooped his big hand full of the mixture on the tray and sipped from the cup, waiting for the Chief to say why he had asked him to come.

"Growling Bear, I have been thinking about our poor attempt at having games to make a fence for our herd. I think it is time to do it. Don't you?"

"Yes of course I do and we have more men now to help with the work of it. We still have the things we had planned for prizes and I even have the bundle of sticks for measuring the depth of the post holes. All we need to do is go in the woods and mark the trees again for the rails and posts. I am sure that the weather has erased those long ago."

"I think we should hold the men's fence building games the morning after the next rain," said Chief Dark Wolf. "I will send White Grass to tell all the men that they should plan on participating. In the meantime you can get a few men to gather stones to replenish the first pile. We used a lot of it to cover Father Pete's grave."

"It is good. Thank you my Chief," he said as he left. He went straight to Night Hawk. "Do you think we should still do the log roll at the end?"

"Yes I do. Flying Eagle is as arrogant as ever."

"Since the Abalinah came, I haven't been working at my stone throwing and log rolling. I think I better go for a walk this afternoon and make sure I still can hit my marks. It has been more than a year."

Growling Bear worked at building his strength up each day. He carried most of the stones to the pile himself not asking for help. The late fall days stayed hot and dry. He became more eager than most for the rain to come. He wanted the games to begin. The women had harvested the corn and the night guard had held two monthly meetings and each time their assigned positions were changed. Growling Bear played with his growing sons, and helped Big Flower to add skins to their tent. They were not seeking status by increasing its size. They simply needed the room. He liked the new positioning of the tents; it put him close to all his hunters and warriors.

Since the weather stayed dry, he decided to take some of his hunters and see if they could come back with some more meat for winter. The few buffalo they had seen had not returned. With Chief Dark Wolf's permission, he took only the youngest hunters. He planned to work on their scouting and tracking skills.

The seven men headed out through the big rock country, glad to be relieved of their guard duties for a few days, the young men, inexperienced and overly enthusiastic, were eager to prove themselves.

"Which direction do you think we should go?" he asked casually as they stopped on the edge of the prairie, giving their horses a drink from the big crocks of water hidden in the shade of the last big rocks.

"I know it is a long way to go but with it being so dry, I think we are more apt to see game along the Hickory River. There are lots of trees along it for them to find shade and good grass."

"It is your idea, so you lead the way, Two Feathers. See if you can find us a game trail," said Growling Bear. They rode at an angle, heading toward the tall grass area, but he didn't lead them into it.

"After a rest for our horses, we need to keep going to the river," said Two Feathers. He slowed his horse studying the dry grass. A small herd of horses has passed this way. He pointed at their tracks. "Let's try the other way." He turned his horse to the right and then slowly walked their horses on the periphery of the trees. "Let's stop and rest and let the horses enjoy the sweet grass near the water."

The men had a lunch while their horses rested and grazed on the water's edge.

"We should get moving," said Growling Bear. All the young men instantly responded. They respected him and wanted to please him.

As they rode along, Two Feathers watched the ground for prints of any kind.

"I see the prints of horses again, these have shoes on them. It looks like they stopped here. It might have been a family. It looks like a woman, man and a third, another woman or big child. They all entered the water here then turned around and went back."

"Why would they come here to go in the water? They could swim or fish anywhere along the river?" asked Pine Berry.

Growling Bear got down from his horse and studied the footprints leading to the water.

"There is nothing here that is different. They may have been people looking for land to settle. So far we have not seen the track of a deer or even a rabbit run. Let's move on. The shadows grow long. Sometimes this is when the deer graze in the open."

He swung up and moved out and so the others quickly did the same. Two Feathers held his hand up to stop and silence the group. A head of them stood a large buck with a big rack. Beside him were two younger deer with small spike antlers. Growling Bear indicated that Two Feathers should take the largest deer. He motioned for Pine Berry to aim for the deer on the right and for White Grass to try for the one on the left. He gave the signal and one deer slumped to the grass. Two Feathers had been successful.

"That was an accurate shot Two Feathers, he said smiling and praising the young hunter. White Grass and Pine Berry, go find your arrows. You will do better next time.

After the deer was cleaned and tied onto a travois, they moved on a short way and then camped for the night in the edge of the tall grass.

During the night, Growling Bear heard a small sound that was different from the sound of the wind moving the grass. He readied his bow, turning to watch the area where the deer lay covered on the travois. The wolf pawed at the hide covering the meat and then tugged it aside with his teeth, as the young men slept

177

soundly a short distance away. Growling Bear continued to wait until a second wolf appeared, the first one growled possessively. It was then that the experienced hunter placed a swift arrow in the heart of each, quicker than the blink of an eye. Still the young men slept.

After pulling the wolves a few feet away, he covered the deer again with the hide and laid back down. They can skin them in the morning he thought.

At first light, he nudged the young hunters and asked who had shot the wolves. They scrambled to their feet, moving away from the wolves as they came fully awake. Growling Bear laughed until his sides hurt.

"You are night guards? I hope you stay awake at your positions because you all sleep soundly when you go to sleep. These two came for a free meal. You two didn't get a chance to clean a deer so you can practice on my wolves. My sons will have warm coats this winter."

With the job done, the hunters headed home.

"How did you know they were in the tall grass," asked Debon?

"I heard the first one coming and it is common for a second younger wolf, or a female with nursing cubs, to follow the path of a good hunter."

"This was fun," said Spotted Feather. "I hope you will choose to take us again soon." Just then he held his hand up. They all stopped; watching as the deer walked slowly out of the woods and walked toward the tall grass. Spotted Feather was ready with his arrow, but Growling Bear nodded for Debon to try. His arrow grazed the shoulder of the deer as it leapt. Spotted

Feather had anticipated its jump and downed the deer with a perfect shot.

"Flying Eagle told me to watch their hind muscles and to shoot ahead of them if they start to bunch up. This is my first big deer. He will be proud."

"You did well."

"Debon, help him clean the deer and rig a travois. The rest of us need to get Two Feather's meat back so it can be processed." Growling Bear did not want to hear about the way Flying Eagle was training the young man. I did not want Flying Eagle with us, but still he intrudes, thought Growling Bear with resentment, as he moved toward the big rocks. Falling Stones greeted them. He was covering the guard position at the start of the path.

"I see your young hunters were successful!"

"Yes and Spotted Feather follows with another. He is cleaning it now. Debon is with him. They should be here soon."

After they entered the camp many of the seasoned hunters made the effort to stroll over and praise the accomplishment of the young men. It wasn't until then that Growling Bear told them that they were to make racks and process the meat themselves.

"This is a skill that all men need to know. You should all help and share the dry meat when it is ready to be stored. Two Feathers, I know it is tempting to have Willow help you, but she is not to touch it. The man who shot the animal may keep the hide, but he must also preserve it himself. It was a good hunt, men. I am proud of all of you."

Growling Bear rode behind the tents. He spotted Bending Grass and motioned for him to come. At his tent he then instructed the lad to remove his gear from the horse and to take the horse to the back of the lake and release it.

"Yes Growling Bear, it is an honor." Bending Grass did as he had been instructed. He was eager for the day when he would be allowed to go with the young hunters. One more year and I will take my three day journey, he thought.

Growling Bear smiled as he entered his tent. Big Flower had rearranged the inside of the tent. Their three young sons were all napping on pallets that she had placed along the back wall end to end.

"You have moved things. I like it," he said giving her a quick hug. "It gives us more room here in the front to sit and talk or eat inside if it rains."

"I wish it would rain. Everything is dry and dusty," she said. "Were your young men able to find a deer?"

"They brought back two. They will be tired by the time the meat is in their caches. They won't have to stand guard tonight, but tomorrow night they will."

"If all is well, tomorrow morning I plan to take the rest of the night guard out for a hunt. Have you got all that you need before I leave?"

"You are a good provider. We have all that is necessary, but we all miss you. Cub misses you. I wish that one of the other hunters could take the young ones so you could be here with us."

"I am top hunter! I train the new men, no one else! He stormed loudly, waking the babies.

"Of course you are, she said. "Don't get upset. I just meant we miss you when you are gone," she whispered, patting the twins and hoping they would go back to sleep. Growling Bear picked up Cub and said he was going to see the Chief.

Chief Dark Wolf and Sky Fire sat with willow backrests in the shade of a large old tree. They both smiled when they saw him coming with the little boy.

"Growling Bear I heard that the young men have been successful in the hunt.

"They have two deer. I would like to take the rest of the night guard in the morning and give them a chance."

"That is fine, but are you sure you want to leave again so soon? Big Flower will not be happy with your absence. You know how women are. You could assign one or two of the seasoned hunters to take them."

Cub squirmed to get down and chugged over to the Chief; touching the beaded breast plate that he was wearing. The men laughed at his efforts. He is a born leader, Growling Bear. He already reaches for the symbol of authority." Growling Bear snorted at the comment and scooped up his son.

"One day he will lead the hunters as I do now, if there is anything left to hunt!"

"Yes I think Bending Grass or Walking Tall will be able to carry a message if it is necessary. Take your young men, if you feel you should."

"Thank you my Chief."

He did not take the boy immediately back to his mother, but instead he walked down the path passed the lake, scooping water up for the boy to have a drink and then he had Gray Cloud pull a gentle horse from the herd for him.

When he saw the boy's bare legs, Gray Cloud covered the back of the horse with his own blanket and slipped on a soft bridle he had used earlier. Growling Bear thanked him and slid up easily with Cub in his arms. He headed to the far end of the meadow moving slowly. He placed the boy in front of him and put the reins in his small hands, placing his own on top.

"Where would you like to go Cub? We can go in the woods in the shade if you want."

He directed the horse with his knees and enjoyed the time with nothing more required of him than to spend time with his little boy.

Big Flower was sitting with the twins under the shade pavilion with the story mothers. She had seen Growling Bear take Cub for a ride and was very pleased. He returned with a hungry, wet boy in need of his mother. Growling Bear traded Cub for a baby on each arm and walked back to their tent with her.

"I have packed your food for your trip tomorrow and filled the water bag. Your meal is ready if you are hungry. We have buffalo meat with mushrooms and onions and I made crackers and greens to go with it. I had to use dried greens. It is so dry that the ones on the prairie are harsh and bitter. The old women tell me that their bones ache. They say it will rain tomorrow. If it does, will you go hunting in the rain?"

"No. I hope it does rain then we can hold our fence building games. The Chief said the day after our next rain we can start the games. All the men know about it and are eager to begin."

"I think it will be a lot of fun to watch. We have many strong men in camp now. More than we ever had before."

Growling Bear took his group of young hunters out through the big rocks at first light, but the sunrise was just a lightening of the gray sky. He warned them that it might be a waste of time.

"Animals bed down when it rains. They seek the shelter of dense pines or heavy brush where they are protected from the wind. We can search the edge of the woods but the chances aren't good that we will see anything grazing."

A loud clap of thunder overhead helped him to decide to take his hunting party back to their tents.

"Rest up if you can because if it rains, remember that the games start the next morning." With that instruction he led his group back to camp and was surprised to find a men's meeting had been called and any man that wasn't at a guard position was in the big tent.

"What's going on?" he asked a boy that ran past him.

The boy shrugged and kept going.

When he entered the tent he knew that it wasn't a meeting of the usual nature. Chief Dark Wolf lay in the corner on a pallet of furs and Sweet Water hovered near, pressing wet cloths to his face. He doubled up in pain and his face grew white. She offered him willow bark tea but he refused it. She pressed gently on his stomach first one place and then another. When she pressed, he screamed in pain. Her hands shook as she backed away from him.

Moonflower knelt nearby, looking worried.

"We need Father Bob!" She said softly. He must ask the Great Spirit to save our Chief. I cannot help him. Walking Tall ran to the church and interrupted Father Bob's meal.

"Come, you must come now! The Chief is very ill. You must come pray!" He shouted his message and headed back to the big tent, followed by Father Bob, just as the rain began.

By the time they got in the tent both of them were soaked to the skin. Father Bob thought that this was another test of the people's faith and of his. He knelt near the Chief and asked everyone else there to kneel. He turned to Moonflower and asked her what he had eaten in the last few hours.

"I made buffalo meat with dried mushrooms and onions. I took some of it to Big Flower. It was good. We all ate it last night. I didn't cook this morning. He finished the leftovers."

"So he ate it twice?"

"Yes and all the mushrooms."

Big Flower burst into the big tent with Cub in her arms. He was screaming wildly.

"Sweet Water, help him. He is very sick!" The boy's face was red from crying and his little chin quivered as his stomach cramped.

"What did you feed him?" asked Sweet Water.

"I fed him some soft meat and the rest of the mushrooms and some crackers."

"When?"

"A little while ago, he liked the meat so well last night that I let him have the rest of it this morning."

Moonflower covered her mouth to stifle a cry.

"It was the food I made." She started to cry. Sweet water sprang into action dissolving a large quantity of salt in warm water. She added an herb and a handful of the precious sugar they obtained from the trading spot. She stirred it as it heated. She poured some in a cup and handed it to Big Flower.

"Make him drink it all and take him outside. He will empty his stomach and be better." She carried a large cup to the Chief.

"You must drink this. It will make you empty the poison from your stomach. Please help him outside."

As she worked Father Bob had been praying asking God to help Sweet Water. He continued to pray out loud and then stood.

"Come all of you that are not sick, follow me to the church." He led them through the downpour to the small church where they interceded for their Chief and the little boy. They prayed and waited. Finally word came. They were doing better. Father Bob started Mass then, knowing that the Great Healer had once again showed the people His power and grace.

CHAPTER THIRTEEN
LET THE GAMES BEGIN

Chief Dark Wolf tried to comfort Moonflower. She had gathered the mushrooms in the same location they had found some on other occasions. She had not noticed any difference in their appearance.

"I don't understand why we didn't all get sick. Growling Bear ate some and so did I," said Big Flower.

"We ate some of the meat out of it last night, but not very much. We wrapped it in corn cakes."

"I am so sorry Big Flower. I was just trying to help you."

"I know you were. Cub is going to be fine and the Chief is feeling much better too."

*****

The women had all gathered on the grass hill, sitting on oiled hides or old blankets. The church stood behind them and Father Bob, Night Hawk, Snapping Turtle and Growling Bear had explained the rules to everyone. The first challenge was to have six post holes dug the fastest. The teams each held one shovel and one measuring stick. The hole had to be as deep as the stick was long and large enough to place a foot in and stand on it in the bottom. Growling Bear brought down the yellow cloth and the digging began. The women could hear their men laughing and shouting as the work proceeded.

Finally one team hooted and yelled. They had finished the sixth hole. Snapping Turtle inspected the work of the teams as he walked along the zigzag line drawn in the dirt with crushed white stone. Night hawk stepped into each hole made by the team that finished first and declared that they were good. Everyone cheered. Thirty Six more men took their places in the assigned teams and locations. Some were young and some were old. No one was turned away, but wisely Growling Bear tried to balance the teams out with men of similar strength on each team.

The yellow cloth went down again and the dirt was flying. The men worked farther down the meadow now but the women could still see the progress as shovels were quickly handed to the next man. By the end of the day, each man that was participating had dug four holes and the herd would not be allowed back on the meadow until posts and rails were in place. Night Hawk checked the lines that held the horses surrounding the lake. He didn't want any of them getting loose and stepping into a hole and breaking a leg. Gray Cloud, Coyote, Singing Wind and Falling Stones had taken the initiative to cut great bundles of grass and as the area around the lake became sparse from overgrazing, they distributed the grass as needed to the horses tethered there.

At the summer meeting Bezalel had shown several of the Blue Stone men how to easily cut and punch out the posts so they would receive the rails and hold them securely. Now that knowledge was put to use.

Each day a different activity offered an opportunity for the men to gain points toward getting a prize on the last day. Growling Bear had worked on the teams as often as all the others. Flying Eagle had cut and carried more posts than anyone else, but Growling Bear had accurately cut railings and split them cleanly. His pile was the largest.

As the posts were carried and placed in the holes the real competition of strength began. Growling Bear stood beside the first big pile of rocks. He picked up a modest sized rock and threw it accurately against the post about thirty feet away. Men standing near quickly tucked it down to the bottom and stepped back. Clunk, went a second and a third. They wedged those in and backed up as he threw two more, first with his right hand and then his left. Each hit the post. Everyone cheered. He picked up a little larger size rock and as he tossed it, Flying Eagle snorted, distracting him. He cackled as it bounced a little left of the post. Three more thrown quickly, right, left, right, landed within inches of the post and were stomped tightly against it by the men standing near. Lastly, three large rocks needed to be added to secure the post. Quickly he sent them so close that the people were amazed and applauded.

One man after another did their best to match Growling Bear's performance. Distance from the rocks to the post was accurately measured. Rails were dipped in pinesap and tapped into the carefully made holes to join them before they were tied with cord. As the stone throwing continued, the fence grew beside them.

As the strong gate was finished and pushed closed on the path to the big rock area, a loud cheer filled the air. Gray Cloud and Singing Wind opened and closed it several times showing their joy and amazement. The people cheered and the women encouraged their tired men as the fence met the place where the second gate was installed on the path from the lake to the meadow. A final cheer went up and the applause was loud and long.

Father Bob gave a signal and three horsemen led pairs of work horses, from the woods behind the lake. Each pair dragged a long fat log to the base of the hill in front of the church. The women took their children and blankets and moved to the sides where they could see what would happen next.

Only three men knew about this game and its real purpose. Father Bob had been enlisted only as the one to signal the men to bring out the logs. He had no idea what this was really about.

The first muscled team of horses dragged a log that had been greased and rubbed with sand. Around each end a strip of bright yellow cloth had been tied.

The second team pulled a mud caked log with red strips tied on each end.

The third log was clean and tied with blue cloth.

Once all the logs were positioned, the big horses were the first to be release into the newly fenced meadow. As they trotted in through the gate another cheer went up. The people were puzzled by the logs and their position in a row at the bottom of the hill, facing the church door.

"This is our last game. It is a surprise for the men that have already won a prize in the fence making games. Night Hawk has received the beautiful hunting knife with the silver and blue stone decorations on the handle. His prize was awarded for the post hole digging.

Many men worked hard the last four days, and we are proud of all of them. Night Hawk, please stand on the path, by the yellow log." The people patted his back or shoulder as he walked past them. They applauded and cheered. He proudly took his position and bent pretending that he could roll the huge log with one hand. Everyone laughed at his antics.

"Flying Eagle, you have cut and piled more posts than any other man here. You are strong and your youth serves you well. We are proud of your work and you have won the prize of a beautiful breast plate with excellent craftsmanship. It is beaded with bone, shells and the blue stones of our people. We know you will wear it proudly!" The people erupted in loud praise and approval for him and the beautiful prize. "Please take the position on the path, in front of the red log." Flying Eagle started to take his place and then stopped. He looked at Growling Bear and then Night Hawk and Snapping Turtle. All three men were looking very seriously at him. There was no way he could get out of the position he was in. He was sure that the red log had been soaked for a long time. Making sure he would think that, they had arranged to have water poured on the ground along the length of it, while the people were entertained, by listening to Night Hawk announce Growling Bear's prize.

"I am proud to say that Growling Bear has won the prize for rail splitting and piling and the stone toss! The prize is a very special bow, purchased from a soldier at the fort. The balance and strength of it will aid him in leading our hunters for many years to come."

Snapping Turtle had managed to slip into Flying Eagle's tent during the days after the earthquake and studied his hidden bow.

After Sarah's wedding and departure the next morning, he had ridden to the fort and traded for a matching bow.

Now there was no need for a challenge at archery. Flying Eagle recognized that he and Growling Bear had equal skills in that area. He had hoped that his bow would give him the edge that he wanted.

Growling Bear walked smiling, to the spot in front of the log decorated with blue cloth strips.

"Well, do you wish to speak?" Growling Bear looked into the eyes of a man that now hated him. Flying Eagle slowly walked up the hill toward the church until he turned and stood facing all the people of the village.

"Chief Dark Wolf and my people, I have done an evil thing. I must confess my plan to cheat by soaking a log to make it very heavy. I had my friend mark it red so I could easily tell which log. We were planning on making sure that Growling Bear would have the red log, at the log roll at the summer meeting. I am sure that the red log here has been soaked to make me fail, so that I would have to confess. I was glad that we couldn't go last year, because it was then that we had planned to do it. I hope that you can all forgive me and that Snow Star forgives me for the shame I have brought upon her. My Chief, I am so sorry. I will accept any punishment you feel appropriate, but please do not banish me from our people."

It was silent. The Chief walked over to the red log and gave it a hard shove. It rolled a little ways up but rolled back down and settled where it had been.

"Flying Eagle, none of these logs have been soaked. Your guilt has convicted you. We will talk later. I do not want this confession to be a stain on our day of victory. I want to see all our horses in the meadow. Anyone who wants to should untie one and lead it in through the gate! I think some of our women would like to do it. Go ahead, any of you that wants to, may take a horse into the new fenced meadow." Within a few minutes the horses were happily grazing in their meadow.

"Now that is a beautiful sight!" he said. "Gray Cloud, it is clever how you and Singing Wind have dug a small pool fed by the lake, which provides water to the herd inside the fence. I feel that today is a victory for all our herdsmen, Falling Stones and Coyote, too. I still want to hear that beautiful flute music but now when you are not training new horses, you will only need one man on duty. You should work out your own schedules, just keep me informed."

The Four men beamed with his praise and looked forward to more time for their families or hunting or their favorite craft.

Flying Eagle walked over to Snow Star and looked at her questioningly. She lowered her eyes and slowly carried Watching Owl to their tent. She didn't want to say a word where it could be repeated. They would talk privately.

Hondor stood looking down at the three logs in a row and thought that surely it was a waste not to play the game. He had been unaffected by the emotional and humiliating confession of Flying Eagle. In his mind the only fault was admitting a good plan that had failed. The people had drifted away from the sight and he felt that now he had a better chance than ever. Flying Eagle will never be held in high esteem again, although it did take a lot of courage for him to face the whole village.

*****

Hondor had instructed Okallah to slice and cook the poisonous mushrooms. He had carried them in a large cup and quickly added them to the pot in front of Moonflower's tent as he walked by. He hadn't known that she would share the food with Big Flower. It is a shame I didn't add more. We could have gotten rid of Chief Dark Wolf and Growling Bear both at the same time. Another good plan gone badly, he thought.

As he noticed the women making big pots of various foods he realized that the camp would have a communal feast that evening to celebrate the completion of the fence. I doubt if anyone will be cooking anything with mushrooms in it for a while, he laughed to himself. I need to go see what Okallah and Gamier are fixing. He watched Willow walk toward the lake, holding Water Bug's hand. She is filling out in all the right places, he thought. I need to think about replacing my first chosen. It is always a good thing to have more than one woman to take care of a man, he considered her a likely candidate.

Chief Dark Wolf had strolled out onto the meadow. He still felt weak from his bout with the bad food, but he had thoroughly enjoyed the fence games until Flying Eagle's confession. Now he was forced to deliberate on an appropriate action. I have to consider how this is affecting Snow Star. Moonflower is distressed, too. His worse fear was that I would banish him. He knows that our people have never tolerated dishonesty in any form. No matter what I decide this has already had an emotional impact on the people. I have to look at this as if he were not my son-in-law. This is a lesson he must learn well if he is to be the person shaping the future of our people.

He went to his own tent.

"Moonflower, would you mind if I rested for a while? I want to close the flap on the tent and just lie and think."

"Why would I mind? That is a good idea. You were very sick last night and then the games this morning, that was stressful. I am not cooking a thing for the feast tonight. I am tired, too. I think I will rest with you." She tied the flap shut as if she were sealing it permanently. She knew he needed time and didn't want him to be bothered. She edged her furs away from his a little as she smoothed them. She wanted to give him room so that she would not disturb him, if he managed to fall asleep. She also was thinking about Flying Eagle's confession and wondered if anyone else in camp was pretending to be something or someone that they were not. She still was not comfortable around the Abalinah. She understood the Choyinaw a little. Even though they were very different, they were trying to imitate the ways of the people. She believed that they had suffered great pain and loss. Worry crept into her mind as she examined her feelings about the Abalinah. Great Spirit, you see the hearts of the people. If others in our camp are being deceptive please expose them before they can do harm. She closed her eyes and she was able to relax as she heard the steady breathing of sleep coming from Dark Wolf.

Later as the fire was built up and the people were starting to gather, Moonflower heard their voices and tied the flap of the tent open. She was surprised at the sudden chill she felt in the air. She reached for her favorite blanket and wrapped it around her shoulders. Morning Dove was coming around the back of the big tent carrying a heavy tray. Blue Stone followed her with Happy Song toddling along beside her.

Morning Dove smiled broadly and Moonflower gave her a hug, appreciating the much needed support that she always received from her best friend.

"I love the way all the tents are arranged now. I am close to you and Blue Stone and the big tent. It makes life a lot nicer."

"Morning Dove, thank you for being the first person I saw when I looked out. I feel very tired today. I did not cook a thing for the feast."

"We always have so much left over that no one will even notice," Morning Dove assured her.

"They might not want to eat it anyway if they knew I made it." They laughed together easily and Moonflower felt better being in her company.

They sat chatting, sitting on one of the many logs pulled near the big communal fire.

Since the Chief had insisted on the relocation of the tents, people had decided that they could change where they sat at the communal fires. The atmosphere was less formal and seemed more like a celebration when they gathered for a feast.

Snow Star and Flying Eagle's tent had been laced tight since they had entered it earlier in the day. The tones of muffled arguing had been heard but now it was quiet.

Finally Snow Star stepped out and Flying Eagle was seen holding his son close for an instant before handing him to his mother. Flying Eagle added two bundles to his horse and a full water pouch and then walked through the center of camp with his head down. He led his horse that he always kept behind his tent through the gate and Gray Cloud closed it after him without saying a word. Flying Eagle rode to the far gate at the big rocks; closing that gate, he disappeared onto the path through the rocks. Many people had watched him go, but none commented. Snow Star did not attend the feast.

Chief Dark Wolf had stepped out of his tent just in time to watch his son-in-law leave the camp and cross the meadow. He was puzzled and concerned for his daughter, but in a way he felt relief. He would talk with her tomorrow. This could help shape his decision.

Father Bob attended the feast, and stood for just a moment, long enough to say how much he liked the fence and that he had enjoyed taking part in the work of building it. He had considered giving a sermon on honesty, but decided it was too soon. They had all had a pointed lesson on it that very morning.

It was oddly quiet around the fire that night. The men were especially tired and the women seemed to speak in hushed tones.

Chief Dark Wolf knew that he was expected to speak. He always did. He wished he didn't have to. He stood and looked around at his people and for the first time, he became fully aware of the people sitting in seats of their choice rather than status.

"I rearranged the tents, not the people living in them. It seems that you have all done that." He said it lightly and the people laughed. "Is everyone comfortable?"

They laughed again and nodded.

"I see some of you are sharing blankets around your shoulders. I think winter is not far away. I am happy to say that our herd is safely fenced in and won't need anyone sitting out in the cold wind to keep them here, this year."

The people applauded.

"I would like to make a suggestion. Before it snows, I think we should build or make a tent or cover against the trees so that our horses are protected from the worst of the winter snows. It would offer shade in the summer. I would like you all to think about it and then we can have a meeting to talk about our ideas." He sat down feeling exhausted. What is the matter with me? I rested this afternoon. Moonflower looked over at him and realized that something was wrong. She slid closer and asked if he was ill.

"No, I just feel very tired."

"You need to eat something. Let's start the meal so everyone can eat."

Father Bob took that as his chance to pray with the people. He blessed the food and thanked God for the bounty and then he asked a special blessing on the wounded hearts of the people.

"I discern a deep pain in the hearts of some of our people and I ask the Great Healer to come and pass among us right now and to touch those who need it. Lord let your love begin to heal the wounds that some of our people carry in their hearts." One of the children began very softly to sing the Alleluia Holy, Holy, and soon others joined in and before long the camp was filled with the voices of the people praising God. Moonflower's eyes spilled tears on her cheeks as she quickly left the gathering and walked to her daughter's tent, knowing that Snow Star was counted among the wounded.

The next day was cool and breezy. Corn Silk and a few other hardy women left camp and walked the outside edge of the meadow fence to the far woods, carrying gathering baskets.

Father Bob saw them go but decided he didn't want to tag along this time. He spotted Walking Tall and asked him to spread the word that he would hold story time in the big tent that evening and that he would be bringing a treat.

The women returned with their baskets full of apples and nuts. When he saw the bounty he wished he had gone. He promised himself that he would go soon.

He had been working all day cleaning the inside of the church and replacing the grass bundles under his sleeping furs and some from the main part of the church. Tall grass was harder to gather this fall because the horses had done a very good job of cropping all the grass near the lake and back of the church, while they were tethered there during the building of the fence. The crumpled grass from inside, was given to his mules and Father Pete's horses to enjoy. He found by following the fence toward the big rocks, He could cut and roll the tall grass and it wasn't that much harder than before. He wanted to be sure that he had enough to make their area comfortable in the coldest months.

As his supply of hides increased, he had made a lining for his sleeping cubicle and now he packed grass between it and the split log walls. He made a leather door for his private area similar to a tent flap. It felt cozy when he stepped inside and dropped it down. The space that had been used by Father Pete was lit from the lantern that hung on a hook overhead. Father Bob had made a rustic table and stool that he could use for reading. I wish he was still here, he thought. It is lonely without him. With a big sigh, he went back outside to make a large batch of sugar candy for the story time in the big tent.

Suddenly he realized that he needed provisions for winter. He needed lamp oil, and other things that he couldn't provide from the surrounding area. All my mules and Pete's horses need shoes. I need to make a trip to the settlement, before the weather gets any colder. I think I should go in the morning. Maybe I will ask one of the young men to go with me.

Father Bob was pleasantly surprised by the number of people waiting for him in the big tent. He had prepared a lesson on marriage, fidelity, and honesty. The Blue Stone People agreed with everything he said, some of the new people thought that he was unmarried because he had strange ideas about how life was to be lived.

Hondor boldly asked him.

"Why do you live alone? Why have you not chosen a woman from the village?"

"I am a Catholic Priest. We do not get married."

"Just choose one to work and to do what you tell her. You do not need to marry her. I am not married."

"Hondor, I would like to talk about this some more, but it is getting late. I plan to leave early in the morning. I need to go to the settlement to buy a few things before winter. If any man would like to go along, I would enjoy the company. He waited, but no one accepted his invitation. He gave each person a generous piece of the sugar candy as they filed out. Moonflower had provided crackers and honey to go with the tea that Sweet Water had made. It had been a pleasant evening.

"Chief Dark Wolf, may I speak with you for a moment? I don't like to ask but would you give me enough of the blue stones to pay for my supplies and for getting my mules and horses shod?"

"Please wait here," was his reply. He quickly returned from his tent with a small leather pouch bulging with small blue stones.

"Use what you need and hold the rest for future use. We used to have a shaman that took a share of everything we brought into camp. We shared meat and grain, nuts and hides and furs. Now you are our Holy Man. It is right that we share with you. You provide your own food and I am sorry that you had to ask. It is your due. We appreciate all that you do here. Our new people needed to hear your message tonight. They have some strange ways that I don't agree with. We must work to change them before it becomes a big problem."

"Thank you Chief Dark Wolf and I want you to know that I am praying for your daughter and Flying Eagle. I know God will work it all out for their good."

Chief Dark Wolf gave a small nod and said that he hoped that the weather held so that Father Bob would have a good journey.

CHAPTER FOURTEEN
THE SETTLEMENT

Father Bob had talked to Night Hawk and then Snapping Turtle. He wanted to be sure of his route once he got out on the prairie. He felt at peace as he traveled across the wagon trail and headed at an angle toward the Hickory River, not yet noticeable. It wasn't long before he could see the very distant line of green. The trees that lined the river were huge and could be seen from a long way off.

He stopped often to offer the animals a drink from the generous supply in the water bags he had brought. He had his biggest cooking pot to use for that purpose. He didn't need to carry feed for them because the prairie was covered with ripe wild grain for their nibbling pleasure. He had packed a saddle bag full of food for his snacks and was munching on shelled out nuts when he thought he saw movement in the grass ahead. I am not hunting and I do not want one of my animals to fall prey to anything. He felt concern as he moved forward slowly. He was sure he saw movement. What should I do? I don't want to shoot my gun. I think I'll try scaring it away. He pulled his big cooking pan down from Mabel's back and with a rock he started to bang the pan as he moved his caravan forward. He saw the tall grass part as something hurried away. Good. I think I will keep these handy. He continued on until dusk and made camp at the base of a small knoll that blocked some of the evening breeze.

In the morning he discovered that he was passing the start of a deep ravine. He peered down to see if there was a way down, but there didn't seem to be. I guess I shouldn't waste time exploring anyway, he thought as he continued on.

In the distance the trees finally seemed to be getting close and he could see a herd of dark animals to his right, backed by a woods.

Someone must live near here. They wouldn't just leave these animals unattended, he thought as he passed between the fence and the river. It was kind of them to make a way for a traveler to go along the river and not have to go all the way around their field. Those are mean looking cattle. I don't like riding so close even though there is a fence between us. He stopped long enough to study the channel that took water to the pond for the cattle. Planks had been fastened together to cover it in an area wide enough to take a wagon or buggy. Someone has put a lot of work into this. He appreciated the effort.

Adam was on the bluff and had raced to tell Ben when he saw the rider with a string of five animals following him. He was dressed like an Indian, but something about him didn't seem Indian. Ben and David climbed to the lookout and watched for a long time, until they couldn't see him anymore. They sent Adam to give an all clear, and Ben and David rode down to check the cattle and fill the pond. The area was peaceful and the traveler had continued on. Had David seen him up close, he would have recognized Father Bob, but it had been too far.

Father Bob followed the well-worn trail passed the falls and rapids and entered across the bridge on the Silver just as the sun was setting. He had changed to his black robe in the trees before crossing. With his leather clothes folded in his saddle bag, he walked slowly through town and was glad to discover that the general store and blacksmith shop were the first places that he saw. Both places had closed signs in their windows. He led his animals farther down the street and saw the building with the cross on the top and a bell in a steeple. He felt like he had come home. He started up the steps and stopped. A small sign that read "Parsonage" with an arrow pointed to the first house on the side street. He tied his animals where they could reach the water and grass. Someone had thoughtfully place a railing along the edge of the water. He used it as a hitching post.

As usual, Mabel was complaining.

"Yes I know you want me to take the packs off of you, but you need to wait just a little longer. He scratched her ears and talked to her.

He was just raising his hand to knock on the door when it swung open. Reverend Brown was surprised and pleased to see a fellow minister.

"Hello, Welcome. Please come in. Melanie, set another place dear. We have company." Mel peeked around the corner with a big stir spoon in one hand and a baby on her hip. A big smile greeted him.

"Hello, I am Father Bob. I am a missionary and have been living near the Blue Stone People. It has been nearly two years now, since my first visit in this settlement. That was just to ask for directions to the Indian village."

"I am Reverend James Brown and this is Melanie, my wife. Please just call me Jim."

"Thanks, Bob will do for me. Who is this handsome young man?" He is Willie," answered Mel, "and Violet is this little one's name."

"You have beautiful children," he said following Jim to the kitchen.

"Thanks please have a seat at the table and have dinner with us," said Jim.

"This is an unexpected pleasure. I was just hoping to find someone to direct me to a place to stay tonight and where to put my animals until morning."

"After we eat I will help you make them comfortable and you can stay with us tonight. It isn't anything fancy, but you are certainly welcome."

Father Bob enjoyed the conversation and the food. Melanie had a fried rabbit and oven baked potatoes and garden fresh carrots. She served coffee and had baked cookies for desert. He was amused as he watched her give ,give, specially sized cookies to the children. The perfect size for little fingers, and small tummies, he thought. They talked about many things including his trip there.

"I was impressed by the field of cattle that I passed. I didn't see a house nearby."

"They belong to Ben and Mary Slater. You probably know his sister, Sarah. She was raised by the Blue Stone People."

"Really? I didn't know their place was so close. I would like to stop and see them on the way back."

"She is amazing. Without her I think a lot of the people in this settlement would have died. We had a terrible sickness go through. She made medicine and took it to every house."

"She was the healer for the Blue Stone People. She left before I got there, but I have met her. She came back a couple times to visit. She is a very spiritual girl. She came and helped the people of the village after the earthquake. She is a strong leader. People listen when she speaks."

"People in this settlement owe her a lot. Maybe someday they will be able to thank her properly," said Mel. "I need to tuck the children into bed and then I will come back out to do the dishes. Just relax and talk," she said as she poured them more coffee.

After they finished their second coffee, Father Bob, suddenly remember his animals at the railing by the river.

"I am not a very good traveler. My poor animals are still standing with their packs on their backs. It's a wonder that we haven't heard all about it from Mabel! She is the complainer in the group," he said with a chuckle as they walked out together. As soon as she saw him, she started in.

"See what I mean?" said Father Bob.

Jim laughed and then helped to lead the animals to the barn. The packs were few and light weight. There would be more to carry going back.

After a night spent on their couch, Father Bob slipped quietly out to the barn and said his morning prayers there with his animals. He had his packs tied on Jack and Rudy. Mabel stood near them unburdened. Jim stuck his head in and asked if he wanted some scrambled eggs and coffee before he went to meet Mathew Morgan.

"That sounds wonderful. I will be right in." He led them back to the rail where they could again reach grass and water.

Melanie had breakfast ready when he tapped on the back door and let himself in. Violet ran to him and hugged his leg as if he were her long lost friend. He gently picked her up and held her.

"That was quite a greeting. She is a friendly little girl." He placed her on her chair at the table and wrapped a long scarf around her waist and tied it behind the chair as he had seen Melanie do the night before.

"You learn fast Bob. I'm sure you have very little interaction with the babies in the Indian village."

"That's true, but I came from a big family. I have three sisters and four brothers and I was smack in the middle."

"How long has it been since you visited them?"

"I haven't seen them since I entered the priesthood." My father was opposed to me going in the seminary. I thought that once I finished I would go visit, but I was immediately sent out here. I am supposed to educate the Indians and convert them to Catholicism, but to be truthful; I have learned more from them than they have from me. Sarah taught them a lot about God when she was there. They call God, the Great Spirit, but I think that's alright, because he is the Greatest Spirit."

Father Bob smiled as he watched Melanie spooning eggs and mush into her children's mouths.

"They are precious Melanie and you are a good mother. You make it all look so easy. Thank you for the use of the couch last night. My bed is nowhere near as soft, and thank you for all the good food. I am looking forward to the next time I come back so I can see you all again and perhaps mooch another meal," he said laughing."

He had chosen a beautiful piece of turquoise from the leather pouch while he was in the barn. He handed it to Jim.

"I have a gift for Melanie that will require some work from you, Jim. Please polish this and drill it so that Melanie can wear it as a necklace."

"This is beautiful, but you don't need to give us anything. We enjoyed your visit. We don't get a chance to have anyone here very often," said Jim.

"Oh, Bob that is so pretty. Thank you." She held it in her hand as if she thought it would break.

"I hope that Jim has the patience to polish it for you. The men in the village use sand to start and then ash."

He blessed each of the children with the sign of the cross and placed a kiss on the top of their heads.

"I have enjoyed being here with you, more than you can imagine," he said as he walked to the string of animals that he had brought and Jim walked out with him.

"Do you want me to come with you to the blacksmith shop and the store?"

"No Jim, that's not necessary. I know where they are. I am sure that you have things to do and I saw the shops last night as I entered the settlement. I am wondering how long it will take him to get new shoes on all these guys. I want to get down there so he can get started."

"Well, I hope we can see you again soon. It was nice getting acquainted," said Jim.

Father Bob led his string of horses and mules down the street on foot, noting the lovely sound of someone playing a piano. He noticed the crisp white sheets already on a line drying in the early morning sunshine. Two barefoot boys ran by shooting at him with their fingers, imagining they were robbers and their hands held shiny new pistols. He shook his head in dismay. What is this world coming to? He thought. Mabel voiced her grievance with being shot at.

"Well for once I agree with you, old girl," he said laughing as he tied the rope to the rail in front of Matt's shop.

"Good morning Father. You must be new to the settlement. I don't recall seeing you before. I am Mathew Morgan." He held out his strong hand in welcome and shook Father Bob's enthusiastically.

"Hello, I am new. I am just a visitor to Silverville. I am a missionary and have built a small church by the Indian village. I'm Father Bob and I have six animals in need of some tender loving care. They have traveled a long trail and every one of them needs shoes."

"It is nice to meet you Father Bob." Matt had already checked Rudy and Mabel while they were talking and fully agreed that they would need some work. He lifted another foot and saw that Jack's hind hoof was starting to split.

"You didn't come any too soon on these poor fellows. This one would have been limping soon. He is going to need a metal band on this hoof before I can shoe it. I charge twenty five cents for a set of new shoes and it will be an extra nickel for this guy's band. I hope you know that it will take me all day to get this many done correctly."

"Yes, the price is fair and I am willing to wait. I need to go over to the store and I may do some other business while I am here. Take your time. I'll see you later." Father Bob strolled across the street and introduced himself to Sam and Helen. He asked if there was a bank in Silverville and Sam said he was the banker, sort of, and would help if he could.

"I was hoping to exchange a few of these for some cash."

Sam's eyes widened as he saw the beautiful piece of blue turquoise that Father Bob pulled from his pocket.

"That might be something I could help you with," said Sam. "Did you need to buy supplies? Maybe we can trade," he suggested.

"I will be glad to trade, for the supplies I need, but I would like to trade a few for cash, too."

Sam was holding the stone as if he already owned it and he was hoping for a lot more. This looks like it came from the Indians. The Blue Stone People trade for almost anything and what they have looks like this." Father Bob noticed how tightly Sam held the stone and the eager expression on his face.

"I will need several jugs of lamp oil and four lamps. I would like a big coffee pot and three bags of coffee. Also the usual, like sugar, extra sugar, I will need two big bags of that, and flour, salt, and cinnamon. I have six animals but no wagon so I will need the stuff wrapped into manageable bundles. You can add four of the brightest blankets you have and I need a pair of black pants size thirty six by thirty one, and a white shirt, size large. I can use some socks, if you have black ones, I'll take four pair and two of the undergarments, size large. I'm sorry ma'am; I don't want to embarrass you."

"That's fine Father. After all I am here selling these things every day. I am aware of a person's need for undergarments." They all laughed cordially.

He smiled when Henry came in the store.

"Who are you? You sure dress funny," said the youngster boldly. He was one of the lads that had pretended to shoot him earlier.

Father Bob laughed and replied that he was Father Bob.

"Who are you young man?"

"My name is Henry and my father owns this store."

"That's nice."

Father Bob looked at the growing list and added a fifty pound sack of dried beans.

"I don't know if I can sell you that much. I think that will take all the beans that I have in the store," said Helen.

"They won't be wasted," he said casually. "Please get all of the supplies bundled and figure out the cost. Sam, you can hold onto that stone as a partial payment until I come back." Sam had casually tucked the stone in his shirt pocket as he wrote the list. He grinned and said he had forgotten about it.

Father Bob wanted to check with Matt and see how he was doing.

"I decided to start with your three horses. They all need shoes and this guy is getting pretty old. He could do well with a very slow stroll home and a warm shelter this winter. I'm guessing that his back hurts when he has to carry anything," said Matt compassionately. "See those bumps along his spine, the poor old guy."

"I had no idea that he was that old or sore. They were Father Pete's horses and he came out with a wagon train two years ago. He is gone now, so I guess these guys are mine. What do you think I should do for him? Is there some liniment I should rub on, or just let him live out his days free of work. I really don't know a lot about horses," admitted the priest.

"Don't just turn him loose on the prairie. He will have trouble locating water and he will fall prey to a big predator or pack. Just try to be kind and if it is especially cold, he would like a blanket over his back. Just treat him like he is still too young to work, with lots of attention. We all like that."

"Thanks for the advice. I will do everything you suggested. Oh and don't worry if Mabel gets to complaining. She is the talkative one in the bunch."

"I noticed that already," said Matt. "She is the youngest and in the best shape of any of them. Probably you go easy on her because she complains."

"You are right. I guess I do. I never really thought much about it. I am going to walk up the street and I'll be back later. I'm not on a tight schedule."

"Thanks Father Bob, I'll see you later then."

Father Bob noticed the building with a cross on the door and was drawn to it. He opened it slowly and walked in.

He was puzzled by what he saw. Two men sat playing checkers and drinking coffee. There was nothing sacred in sight. One of the men jumped up and went behind a counter.

"Good morning Father. Is there something I can do for you?"

"I saw the cross on the door and thought this was a chapel or church so I stepped in."

"They painted that on the door, years ago when they held service here on Sunday. That was before the folks built the church. It is just up the street there on your left. You must have walked right past it."

"Yes, thank you. I noticed it. What is it you do here?"

"Well as you can see, we play a lot of checkers," they laughed and he continued. "Father this is the land office. If you are twenty one and the head of a household, you can register for one hundred and forty four acres of free land. The map here on the wall shows where there are pieces of land left that aren't taken. Most of the ones near here or on the good side of the Silver are taken. You don't want land on the far side of the Silver. It is poor dirt and turns into a mud bog. That's nasty stuff and good for nothing. We do have some nice pieces farther out on the Hickory, but you would have to know the land to choose. See here where she turns, she runs right in the middle of the pieces. The chartered surveyor drew straight lines no matter what the river did. It makes no sense to me."

"This is a stroke of luck, my wandering in here. I could certainly use a spot for a mission church along the river. Are there any other requirements?"

"Well you do have to improve the land within the first five years."

"What does that mean?"

"You have to build on it and dig a well. Most folks think it needs to be fenced."

"If I build a church instead of a house, would that qualify?"

"Don't know why it wouldn't. It's still a building," he said grinning.

"Who owns the land along there that is marked off?"

"This piece of woods by the bridge is still available, but folks don't want it. There is too much coming and going they say. Now down a bit there is a piece that Slim Parker got. His wife Mary is running cattle on it now. That reminds me I need to speak to them about improvements. Next piece is open yet, but it is rocks on the back part. Jed and Beth Jones own this one here, and then Ben Slater and then Sarah Slater. Farther out is a piece that David Sharpe spoke for a few months back." He pointed with his pencil at rectangles on the map as he spoke. Each had been marked with a large X to indicate they were no longer available.

"I think I'll close my eyes and just poke," said Father Bob and that's what he did. His finger was on a spot next to David Sharpe's when he opened his eyes. "Looks good to me," he said with a chuckle. The clerk signed a paper and had Father Bob sign and then he stamped it and the other man at the checker table came and signed and that was all there was to it.

"I never thought I could get land for a mission church that easily. Thank you gentlemen, and please leave the cross on the door. I like it there. You have done the Lord's work today." The door gave a thud and a jingle from a bell on a string as he closed it behind him.

He crossed a patch of grass and went up two steps to find that he was standing in front of a boldly printed sign. Steak and spirits, it said. He opened the door hesitantly. Not wanting to walk into a place that had a bad reputation. He saw couples sitting at tables with white linens. They were dressed in their work clothes, but respectable. This was a pleasant little café. The only table available was by the front window. He wasn't sure he wanted to be on display while he ate, but a second look told him that he had better sit down while it was not being used.

A menu had been neatly printed on the wall. It listed steak, fried potatoes, chili, rabbit stew, coffee, wild grape wine, well water and free milk for children. He read it again and decided it all sounded wonderful. A gentleman with a big white apron delivered two heavy laden plates to a table across the room and then refilled their coffee cups. He visited two other tables filling cups as he moved closer.

"What you going to have Father?"

"I'll have the steak and potatoes and coffee."

"Good, because I haven't had time to make the stew yet today." He moved swiftly away and disappeared around a doorway. He wasn't gone very long. He returned with a mug of coffee and a plate that held a big slice of thick crusty bread. He plopped down a jar that contained butter with a knife sticking out of it and quickly walked away. He came back to the room only to deliver food for another table and fill water glasses and coffee mugs. His movements were fast and sure. This certainly isn't his first day on the job, thought Father Bob.

He heard his meal before he saw it. The plate was sizzling. The man held it with a pot holder and placed another holder on top of the linen cloth.

"Don't touch this. It's hot," he said, with a matter-of-fact attitude. A fork and steak knife lay near a bright red and white plaid napkin an inch from his fingers. He hadn't seen them placed there. The man once again went through the door and after a few minutes he returned with a tray laden with food for four people seated in the corner. On his way back through he cleared three empty tables and brushed away any sign that they had been used.

Suddenly he returned and was standing next to Father Bob.

"Hi, I'm Cookie. I work five days at the lumber camp and Saturday and Sunday I am in the café. "You like the food?" He asked with an oriental sound in his voice. It wasn't until then that Father Bob noticed the long braid on the man's back and his slightly slanted eyes.

"Hello, I am Father Bob. Yes I like the food. It is delicious. Is this your place?"

"I built it. It took two years. Now I can cook here."

"You must get tired of cooking every day."

"No, not tired, I am happy. You want more coffee?" he filled the mug and hurried back to his kitchen. When he came back, it was to clear the big table in the corner and to slip Father Bob a piece of pastry.

"Not on menu, just for you," he said with a wide smile.

"Cookie, I have a problem. I have these beautiful blue stones, but no money. He held three small stones in his palm, up where Cookie could easily appreciate them.

"Stones, I don't need stones. You go sell stones and bring back fifty cents. Go talk to Tom at lumber mill. He has money. Maybe he will buy stones."

"Where is the lumber mill?"

"It is not far. You can walk. Go that way. You will hear the noise."

"Thank you, Cookie."

"Ah," he said waiving his hand down. I don't need stones."

Father Bob easily found Tom and when he showed him that he had unpolished pieces of turquoise to convert to cash, Tom was more than happy to buy the ten that he showed him. Father Bob had not revealed the quantity of stones that he had to anyone. They chatted briefly and Father Bob realized that the mill would make building a mission, much easier. He paid Cookie on his way back through town.

"I will stop when I come again and I will be sure to have money. Cookie smiled and thanked him.

At the store he offered Sam a choice of stones or money. Sam gladly took the stones. He placed a higher value on them than Tom had, but Father Bob made sure that they both had fair value.

He paid Matt for his work and thanked him for his helpful advice especially about the oldest animals.

When Father Bob headed out of the settlement and crossed the bridge, he felt that he had accomplished everything that he had hoped for and more.

As Mary's cattle came into view he got an idea. He found the big oak that Tom had described and crossed the river on Mabel, leaving the other five animals near the water; tied where they could graze and drink.

Adam was doing his job and had alerted the family before Father Bob got to the crossing. Sarah recognized him from his clothes at a distance and rode to tell everyone that the priest of the Indians had come.

Sarah was very excited.

216

"Father Bob, it is so good to see you. How did you find me? Why are you here? Is everything all right at the camp of the people?"

"As far as I know they are all well and happy. I have only been gone a few days. They were fine when I left."

CHAPTER FIFTEEN
THE VISIT

"Let me introduce you to my family." She recited names until she was sure that his head was spinning. Mary suggested that they all go up to the new house and sit down. They walked the path slowly as Sarah asked about special people in the village.

"We finished the house during the winter and finally moved in last spring," said Mary as they entered the front door. "Ben and Jed made all the furniture that is inside, but none of that was in here when we had Sarah and David's wedding."

Father Bob looked blank and then he looked at Sarah for an explanation.

"David and I have something to tell all of you. We had two weddings. Father Bob married us at the church of the people, on my twenty-first birthday. I wore a traditional wedding dress of the Winahatah. My friend Blue Stone lengthened her dress for me. Then when we came back Mary and Beth had made the beautiful white dress and worked so hard, that we didn't want to disappoint them so that's when David rode to the settlement and brought back Reverend Brown and Melanie and the babies and we had a wonderful wedding in the new house.

David rode through town telling everyone that if they could follow him back, that he and Sarah wanted them to attend. Some couldn't come on such short notice but some did. Sam and Helen closed the store and brought their children. Helen was a woman that I had a difficult time forgiving. She had spread unkind stories about me to most of the people in the settlement, but when I saw her making the effort to come to the ranch for our wedding it changed everything. She said she was sorry and thanked us for helping the people of Silverville when they were very ill. She and I hugged and it changed both our hearts. I hope we haven't hurt anyone's feelings. We were trying to do the right thing."

Father Bob started to laugh and then so did everyone else.

"Twice married is twice blessed," he said. "It is fine Sarah. You look so concerned. I'm sorry that I laughed at you."

"That was a little more than a year ago. It is all good memories now," said Father Bob. "David I understand that you have chosen a piece of land up river. Have you started to build on it yet?"

"No not yet," David replied with a frown.

"I hope I haven't spoiled a surprise or something," said the priest noticing the strange glances between the family members.

"No of course not, but how did you hear that?" David asked.

"I was in the land office this morning and chose a piece to build a mission church on the river. It happens to be the next plot of land down river from yours. We will be neighbors."

"Father, that is wonderful," said Sarah. "We will be glad to help you if we can, when the time comes. When do you plan to start building?"

"We probably won't be able to start for a couple years. I got a chance to talk to Tom at the mill this afternoon and the wood he cuts is reasonable and he will deliver it too when we are ready."

"He is a very good man, Father. His crew cut all the wood for Jed's house and mine," said Ben.

"That's encouraging. I'm not sure how far up river the land is that I chose. I closed my eyes and let God guide my finger on the map and that was it," he laughed.

"Well that's one way of doing it," laughed David. "It's too late today to go see it, but we can ride up that way with you, first thing in the morning," offered Jed. "Father you can stay with us tonight. We will have the room ready in a little while. I am going to go back now with Beth and help her get Lily settled in Johnny's room. Just come on over when you are ready." They stepped out of Ben's house onto the front porch. The setting sun was streaming its golden rays through the posts on the west end.

They could hear Father Bob saying how beautiful the ranch was. Mary had prepared a large stew and they had all eaten just before he had been spotted. Mary wanted to be sure he wasn't hungry before he went over to Jed's to spend the night. She placed the steaming bowl in front of him and poured his coffee cup full. I have a couple pieces of apple pie left if you have room after that stew Father Bob."

"Mary this smells delicious. I am going to gain weight during this trip. I visited with the Reverend and his wife last night and they fed me well, and then as I grew tired walking around, taking care of business in the settlement, I found a nice café and had a steak and fried potatoes a little past noon."

"That Cookie sure knows what he is doing," said Ben.

"Mary, this stew tastes like beef stew."

"It is. One of our cattle broke through the wire and got very tangled. He was cut up pretty bad. There was no way that Ben could safely get him out, so we have enjoyed some fine meals and preserved the rest of the meat for winter.

"I am such a softy that I had a tough time shooting him, but he was in pain," said Ben.

"That reminds me of something important that I need to ask you. Would you be willing to sell me some of those big fellows? The Indians have not seen buffalo on their hunting grounds for a couple years and deer are becoming scarce. They sure would appreciate having the meat to get them through this winter."

"Ben, what do you think?" Mary was looking at Ben and wondering if he said yes, how they would get the cattle to the Indians.

"Father, have you ever worked around cattle?"

"No I haven't but I'm guessing that they aren't as easy as horses to keep track of."

"I don't know if we can find any wranglers in Silverville or not. We planned on selling the beef to the army and I figured that the soldiers would come and get them. Let's pray about it and maybe God will show us a way while we are sleeping."

"Father it was such a nice surprise having you come to the ranch," said David. "We are going to go to our house now. I hope that we will see you in the morning."

"Sarah and David, I will make sure that I see you both before I leave. Sleep well."

"Father if you are ready, I will go with you and we can put your extra packs in Jed's barn and the animals can go in the corral. There is feed available and a big water trough. The weather is so nice they don't need shelter, but the door of the barn is open. They can go in there if they want."

"That sounds perfect."

As they walked along the path to the crossing, David felt that he needed to offer the priest an explanation for the distance between the ranch and his property, but he didn't want to lie so he told the ultimate truth that he hadn't even admitted to Sarah.

"Father I deliberately picked that piece. I love Sarah and her family, but I wanted land that would not become absorbed as part of this ranch. Does that sound selfish?"

"No. It makes perfect sense to me, said Father Bob."

"I want to build something that is ours that we have made and worked for. It won't be easy, but I think we can do it."

"David, I think you and Sarah can do anything. She is an amazing girl. I remember the night that she brought everyone in the village, to the cross as if it were last night. Father Pete was just as astonished as I was. I miss him."

"Did he leave?" David asked.

"He died. He had great chest pain and died nearly a year ago. He hadn't been sick. We buried him beside the church."

"I'm so sorry, Father. I will tell Sarah when I get back."

Beth had thoughtfully prepared a pot of chamomile and lemon grass tea and put the pot of honey on the table. She had thought about the fruitful day that the priest had experienced and knew that if it had been her, she would have a difficult time relaxing enough to rest. She felt a great deal of appreciation for what he was trying to do at the Indian village.

Already she was planning on ways they could help him when the time came. If he opens a mission school there on the river, we could expand the garden a little and take them the extra produce. Maybe I could go down and help teach them our language a couple mornings a week.

Then she thought about Father Bob heading up river to see the land he had chosen. I hope they leave early enough so that the sun doesn't shine on Sarah's rocks. I think I'll make sure they do. She immediately started mixing up a batch of biscuits. With those baked and ready all I need to do is slip a few pieces of sliced beef and some cheese in the bundle and they can stop for a meal along the way. She pulled two water bags from the storage room and filled them. The biscuits were just coming out of the oven when the men stepped in the door.

"Beth that aroma is enough to make me want to eat again. They smell wonderful," said David.

"Now I wish I had not eaten that apple pie," said Father Bob.

"These are for your trip in the morning," said Beth, sliding the hot cookie sheet onto a wooden cutting board to let it cool. "I knew you would want to head out early so I made the biscuits to pack. You can take a snack and stop along the way to eat while your horses rest."

"That's a good idea Beth. I am guessing that Father Bob will want to head home around noon, so he can cover some distance before dark. So far it looks like the clear weather is cooperating. No one likes to travel in the rain."

Ben tapped on the door and stepped in.

"I just checked on your mules and horses. I wanted to be sure they were happy. Your oldest horse is in the barn. He went to the big stall in back and is sleeping curled up like a foal. He is worn out from the trip and being in the settlement. Oh and Sarah came back down long enough to say that she will ride out with us in the morning. She will be at the crossing at dawn. sheShe has packed a few snacks for us."

"It sounds like we are going to have a wonderful picnic," said Father Bob. Since we are leaving at dawn, I think it is time for me to say my evening prayers and get some rest. Thank you Beth, for the tea, I could taste the chamomile in it. I think I needed that. I am still excited about getting the land for the mission church. Good Night and God bless all of you."

"I think I will stay at the ranch and do the morning milking," said David. "We can't all go," he said, "but I will stop in for one of those biscuits with your apple jelly when I am done," he said grinning. "I appreciate all the good things you girls make."

"I'll make sure that I put a couple in the cupboard just for you, David," she said with a smile.

Jed sat at the table sipping a cup of the tea and smiling as David left.

"I wonder if the priest realizes that the river runs through the back of that piece of land, and it is heavily wooded. He will have to do some clearing before he can build."

"I would be willing to help him, if we can at the time," said Jed. He will need some big work horses to pull stumps.

"He needs a good riding horse before then. I checked his animals and all of them are ready to retire, said Ben. I noticed that he put new shoes on all of them. I wondered when he said he was walking in the settlement. That is the reason. He left them all with Matt."

"Do you think he would like Macho? I feel sorry for that oldest horse in the barn. I am going to have him ride Macho in the morning and if they get along well, I am going to give him to Father Bob. If he will exchange him for the old one, he can stay with us and enjoy his last days."

"Ben that is nice of you. I agree that he should have a sound riding horse. Now that he has that land for the Mission Church, he will be going back and forth more. I am sure there are other things that we can help with when the time comes," said Jed.

"What should we do about the cattle he wants for the Indians?"

"I think our best chance is to ask the men at the mill. Maybe some of them would be able to help. Father said he met Tom. If we explain that he is trying to open a Mission School and they have to have the meat for this winter," said Ben, maybe they would be willing to take the time to help with the cattle."

"He can't teach hungry children," said Beth.

"Well that sounds like a play for their sympathy, Beth," said Jed.

"That's alright with me," offered Ben, "as long as I have some experienced volunteers and I don't get trampled by those big beasts. I am no wrangler and I know it."

"Sarah will probably be down there all the time once it is built," said Beth. "Can you believe that pair? Having two weddings and not saying a word until now. She was worried that our feelings would be hurt if we found out that she had married and we weren't there."

"Sarah does things her own way, but it always turns out with a good result. She is a very clever and caring person."

Beth had finished her tea and stood up from the table.

"Tomorrow is going to be a full day of work. I think we all better get some rest. Goodnight Ben."

"I want to check his animals one more time, and I will pull Macho out of the field and put him in the corral so they can all get acquainted. That will speed things up in the morning, too," said Jed.

"Great," said Ben, thanks. Goodnight." Jed watched Ben ride home on Sundown. I think that big guy and his father could pull a few stumps from the land for the mission, thought Jed as he headed for the gate to get Macho.

Josh was still awake and eating the last piece of apple pie and washing it down with milk when Ben returned.

"Hi Dad, we have an all clear, and all the animals are fine."

"Thanks son. Hey I was planning on finishing that pie," he laughed easily. Theirs was a home of bounty and Josh knew that he was being teased. "Are you going to help with the milking in the morning?"

"Sure if you want me too."

"Josh I was checking the entire group of the priest's animals, and they are all getting pretty old. I am thinking that I want to give him Macho if he likes him. I would like to keep the oldest horse here. He needs to retire. He went in Jed's barn and lay in the back stall like a foal and went right to sleep."

"He probably doesn't have a barn where the priest lives. He lives with the Indians, doesn't he?"

"No, I think he has his church on the other side of a small lake. Sarah was telling me about it one day."

"Does he sleep in the church?"

"I am not sure what he does, but I doubt if the horses have a barn."

"Dad, why does he dress like that?"

"That is so that when people see him, they know that he is a Catholic priest. It's sort of like a uniform that a soldier wears. When you see it, you know the man is in the military."

"It seems strange to me, but it's alright. I do understand. Dad, are you going to tell him about the gold in the morning?"

"No, I don't plan to. Why would you ask that?"

"Mom said he got land right beside our gold. I was wondering if he already knows."

"I don't think so Josh. He just picked a piece of land at random on the map. Did your mom tell you that he is going to build a mission school for the Indian children?"

"Yes, but I still feel funny that he picked land so close."

"Josh, I'm tired and we plan to head out at dawn. I guess I can count on you to help David in the cow barn then?"

"Sure Dad, Goodnight."

The house was still and Ben couldn't get his mind off that old horse in Jed's barn. I think I will put him in the field with Dart Away. They can keep each other company and come and go as they choose. With that thought, he was able to fall asleep. He slept soundly and was surprised when Mary opened the curtains and the sun was shining in brightly.

"No need to hurry, Sarah and Jed have gone with Father Bob. They left about an hour ago. Adam wanted to go, but I said no. I was afraid of what he might say or do once they got there. I'm not sure just how much he knows."

"Why didn't you wake me?"

"I needed you here with me today, Ben. You know that old horse that Father Bob brought? He is still in the stall and I didn't want the boys to see him. He just went to sleep and that was it. You knew he was near his end didn't you? He was comforted by the hay and barn. Jed noticed it at first light and he closed the barn door. Johnny and Adam are on the bluff with a treat, but I will call them down and put them to work in our barn when you get ready to move him. David was here and he said he will let you know as soon as they finish the milking. Josh knows and he will help too." Mary noticed that Ben's eyes were watery.

"Don't feel bad Ben. He had a comfortable end." She was trying to console him. He didn't understand why he felt attached to a horse that he had never spent time with until he realized that it wasn't so much the priest's horse that was making him feel bad. He had gotten hold of the fact that any day he could look out the window and it could be Dart Away.

"I'll take care of it Mary," he said. He wrapped his arms around her and held her tightly. "I've never buried a horse before. It's going to take a big hole." He straightened his shoulders and put on a small smile for her. "Give me about an hour to dig it behind Jed's barn and then get the boys down off the bluff."

Father Bob and his companions were back by late afternoon and they were all excited to share their adventure with Ben, David and everyone else.

"You are not going to believe this Ben," said Father Bob, "but we found gold! There is lots of it in the river on Sarah and David's land and on mine. Look!" Father Bob's hands were trembling as he held out several rocks that he had picked from the river where it ran through his land. The little ones look like pure gold and the bigger ones look like there is gold in them. This is why God chose that piece of land! This will pay for the school and a real church and housing for the children and teachers. Oh I am so excited that I can't stand it!" He said it so quietly that they were not sure that they had heard him.

"God is so good," said Sarah.

"Father, we have some news to share with you, too, but I'm afraid it isn't joyous."

"What is it Mary?"

"Your old horse went in the barn last night and went to sleep in the back stall. He didn't wake up this morning. Ben gave him a place in our meadow behind Jed's barn."

"That is a good quiet end for a sweet horse. He was Father Pete's. Now they are together again," he said. "I appreciate you taking care of him for me." There was a pause in the conversation as Adam and Johnny came running in.

"All done," they reported as their eyes fixed on the rocks that Father Bob and Sarah were holding. "Is that gold?" asked Johnny.

"Yes it is. Father Bob has found gold on his property. He has enough to pay for the mission school."

"That's wonderful," said Adam still looking at the gold.

"Ben, Jed told me to ride Macho this morning. I did. He is a smooth gated animal. I would like to buy him from you."

"Sorry Father, but he is not for sale. He is a gift, to help you with the mission."

"Macho is one of many that we caught from a wild herd. He is a good strong fellow and young enough to serve you well for years to come."

"Ben, I don't know what to say. He is a wonderful horse and I like him. Thank you so much for giving me a new friend. I know you have put a lot of gentle work and affection into him. I promise that I will take good care of him."

"Now, as much as I don't want to leave, I think I better get packed up and be on my way."

"Father, stay the night and leave first thing in the morning. You will want to ride on Macho and he is tired after your trip to see the land."

"Jed, I don't want to overstay my welcome."

"You can use the same room, and Beth has a pot of her chili cooking. You can't walk away from that."

"I have bread in the oven," said Mary, "so I need to get back to my house. I will bring it to have with the chili."

"How can I turn down such an offer?"

Father Bob did stay the night and left the following morning, as soon as it was light. The many packs that he had were distributed between Jack, Mabel and Father Pete's two pack horses. Rudy would not have to carry a load. Father Bob explained to Ben and Jed as they helped him settle his packs, that Rudy had brought the cross, all the way.

"He has been a reliable friend. It's time that he retired and I plan on spoiling him this winter. I made a lean-to for all of them, but I think I will extend it and close it in more than it is. Pray that the winter holds off a little longer."

CHAPTER SIXTEEN
BACK IN CAMP

It had been two moons since Flying Eagle left the camp of the Blue Stone People. He had spent most of the time in the camp of the Omati, with his father, Chief Black Thorn and his mother Lady Bee.

They had listened when he told his story and his father had sympathized. His mother did not. She was cross the whole time and finally she told him to come and walk with her.

"Flying Eagle, how could you be so stupid and uncaring? I am very angry with you. You know that this has caused Chief Dark Wolf and Moonflower a lot of worry and pain. Snow Star is angry and hurt. Their own daughter sent you away. Now you have to get back there and find a way to be forgiven by her and everyone else. Chief Dark Wolf will not easily accept you. You must convince him that you will never try to deceive one of the people again. You were in line to be Chief! Now you have been cast from their camp. I feel shame that one of my sons has acted without honor. Have you noticed that your brother stays away from you? If he is not hunting he is in his tent with the flap shut. He too feels shame. Go hunting with him. Talk with him and make it right. Go back to the Blue Stone People and Snow Star. Winter is coming. You need to do it now!"

"You are right Mother. I will talk to Black Cloud now. I think I will go back in the morning. I am sorry that I have shamed you."

He headed back to the camp of the Blue Stone People the next day.

*****

As Two Feathers stood guard, he allowed his mind to drift back to the joyous day that he had seen his family last. That was the day that I left for my three day journey. Father had given me good advice. He said to make sure I found a place of shelter. I was so young then and thrilled to be out on my own. I didn't take his advice, but I see no reason to not take it now. Those clouds rolling in look heavy with rain. He cut pine boughs and made a Shelter just inside the tree line. It was solid and tall enough that he could bring his horse in out of the wind and rain. I can still watch the prairie from inside. I always feel that these outer edge positions are the worst, because we can't see the camp. He added another support post as the wind picked up. This will serve the night guard at this spot for a long time. He strolled out on to the prairie and waved to the man on guard at the start of the big rock path. Then he waved to the man farther down to his left, also posted in the woods.

In the morning I am going to tell the men what I have done and suggest that they all do the same. It would be easy to hide a shelter at each position. Two Feathers had been accepted as the leader of the night guard. Chief Dark Wolf had placed Debon on night guard too, although he had chosen Sheltah. They had no children and his hunting skills were not the best and until he improved them, he would receive a ration of the meat that came to camp, because of his service in the guard. Debon also looked to Two Feathers as a leader. It seemed an unspoken rule that whatever he said was accepted.

Spotted Feather still stood his post at night, but had moved back in with Snow Star and Watching Owl after Flying Eagle left the camp. He felt protective of her. His tent still stood in the row with the rest of the night guard, but it was laced tightly shut and seldom used by him. Chief Dark Wolf approved.

*****

Also heading back to the camp of the people was Father Bob. He had decided that he didn't want to take the gold to camp. He had asked Ben to store it for him. It would be a while before he needed to use it and the less known about it the better. His friends at the S. and J. Ranch had said they were certain that the gold on David's land would stay where it was until he and they had decided on a plan of action together.

Two Feathers and Spotted Feather both identified him when he was a long way out. They waved and smiled, welcoming his homecoming.

When Father Bob returned, the people felt it was cause for celebration. This was the first time he had left them for more than a brief hunting excursion. The women gathered around him and poked and peeked at the things he had brought from the Trading Post. He was amused. How unsophisticated they are. They are genuine and unspoiled.

When the fire was lit and the people began to gather, he knew it was time to give the gifts that he had purchased. One of his bundles held packages of peppermint sticks and cinnamon sticks. He broke the peppermint sticks in half and placed the cinnamon sticks still bundled, in his sleeping quarters. He liked the smell of it. He avoided them being spotted. As it grew dark, he poured some lamp oil into two of the new lanterns, adjusted their wicks and took one in each hand to the communal fire. Chief Dark Wolf was smiling at him and so was Moonflower. They were glad he was back.

"I am so happy to be back with my Blue Stone family," he said. "I have missed all of you." They applauded and cheered. "My journey was successful. I have traveled to the settlement of the white men and have news for you. I have met many new people and made new friends. They were kind and when Father Peter's riding horse died, they gave me a good new horse to ride. His name is Macho and he is strong." The people cheered for his good fortune. I was able to find us a new source for meat. My new friend has agreed to sell us some of his beef cattle. I think they are more difficult to control than horses, but he thinks he can find men that have experience. They will bring the cattle to the start of the big rock country and our men will be able to take them from there as they did the buffalo. Our people will not have a moon of hunger. We will all eat well!" They cheered and applauded loudly. Faces beamed.

It was at that moment that Flying Eagle chose to show himself. He stepped into the firelight and the people gasped and grew quiet. Chief Dark Wolf jerked to a standing position.

"Flying Eagle how is it that you are here?"

"I have returned to ask the people to allow me to come back. I know that I have shamed and hurt my family and all the Blue Stone People. I am very sorry for the way I tried to deceive and I promise I will never act that way again. I have been gone from Snow Star and Watching Owl for two moons. I have learned much in that time. I have learned how important my family and the people in this camp are to me." He stood with his eyes downcast. Father Bob wasn't sure what his role in this scene should be. He felt as uncomfortable as everyone else. He hoped that Flying Eagle's repentance was sincere. He chose to believe that it was. He stepped close to the young man and spoke loud enough for all to hear.

"I forgive you. Jesus forgives our sins when we ask and we should forgive one another." Father Bob wrapped his arms around him and patted his back and then sat down on a mat that Moonflower had provided for him beside her in the spot that a shaman would have been sitting. Chief Dark Wolf was still standing. He looked at his son-in-law and hoped with all his heart, that the young man was being truthful.

"I have missed you," he said. He too patted Flying Eagle's back. Moonflower got up when she saw Snow Star abruptly leave the fire with Watching Owl. She followed her to her tent.

"Snow Star, you must forgive him. You need him to come back. He has been gone a long time. Watching Owl misses him. You miss him. I will keep the boy here. You go talk to him."

"No mother," He needs to come to me, here. I need to hear him say that he is sorry, to me."

"I understand that you have cried many nights, but you must accept his reappearance as a sign that he is sorry."

"I can't. Please take Watching Owl to your tent and feed him. Keep him for me tonight. I don't know what will be said here, but he doesn't need to hear it."

Moonflower had not accomplished what she had hoped. At least she is willing to talk to him, she thought. She didn't take Watching Owl to her tent. Instead she carried him back to the communal fire where Flying Eagle was standing on the periphery of the light, surrounded by many of the men. She walked through them as if they were invisible.

"Your son has missed you," she said as she handed him to his father. Flying Eagle was happy to see the boy and gladly took him smiling.

"He has grown while I have been away."

"Of course he has, that's what babies do," she said smiling. Watching Owl clung to his father and patted his shoulder making a happy sound. He was willing to return to Moonflower when she offered him a tasty morsel from one of the nearby trays of food. He was hungry. She raised her chin and pointed in the direction of their tent where Snow Star waited.

Flying Eagle walked away from the men and toward his tent hoping that he would have the right words to put his family back together.

Chief Dark Wolf knew this would be a difficult time for Growling Bear. He motioned for him to come eat and the two of them started the people feasting. Father Bob inserted a fast prayer of thanksgiving for the food and for the safe return of one of their people.

As the evening progressed and Flying Eagle didn't come back to the fire, Father Bob decided that he would give the lanterns to Chief Dark Wolf and Growling Bear. He too had discerned that it would be difficult for Growling Bear to accept Flying Eagle back as one of his top hunters and warriors.

He had purchased four lanterns. He lit these two from the communal fire and handed one to each of the men.

"These lanterns are for our Chief and top hunter and warrior," He said it with great drama, knowing that the people expected it. "The oil inside will burn down, but I have containers in the church with more so we can refill them. They do get very hot so please put them where they will not burn your tents down. They can be hung high by this wire and it will light a large area. I have brought one to hang in the communal tent and another to light the church." The people thought the lanterns were wonderful. They realized that they would have light without having to have the heat of a campfire on warm evenings.

"That's not all that I have. I brought a new kind of candy!" He had broken the peppermint sticks in half and gave each person a piece. He was saving the cinnamon sticks for another day.

The men of the night guard were irritated. They missed all the fun. As soon as the sun went down they were expected to guard their positions. They didn't get to attend the communal fires or enjoy the feasts.

Two Feathers was glad that the storm had passed over and he had not had to use his shelter. He was surprised when Growling Bear rode out of camp and brought him a lunch from the feast that included a piece of peppermint candy.

CHAPTER SEVENTEEN
NEW LOYALTIES

Growling Bear had been hunting several times in the last two months but he and his men had been unsuccessful. Never before in my life have I seen a time when we could not find some meat in our hunting grounds, he thought. He felt the weight of responsibility to provide for his own growing family, but also he was supposed to be able to lead his hunters to provide for the needs of the camp. He returned to his tent about noon, as promised. It was long enough to tell Big Flower that he wasn't hungry and that she should let him know if she thought of anything she would need in the next few days. He walked through the center of camp and was headed for the Chief's tent when he realized that the Chief was sitting with Father Bob on his little knoll. They appeared to be deeply engaged in conversation.

At loose ends he turned and went to the tent of Two Feathers.

"Two Feathers, are you awake?"

"Yes, come in. What is wrong?"

"Nothing is wrong. I thought perhaps you would like to ride out and see if we can get a deer for Willow's cache."

"If we leave now we will be gone until it is late. I am to stand guard at sundown."

"You are conscientious. We will let the Chief know that you are leaving and I will assign someone to your spot."

"Thank you Growling Bear, I appreciate your thinking of us. It is hard for me to hunt or improve my hunting skills when I must be back and stand guard all night." They walked past the lake and found the little knoll vacant. They pulled two horses from the herd. "We must stop at the tent and tell Chief Dark Wolf," said Two Feathers.

"Now he is in the big tent. I can hear him laughing," said Growling Bear. "Don't worry, it will be fine."

With bundles of food and a water bag on each horse they left camp with rifles and bow and arrows. Growling Bear turned his horse to the right and headed west on the wagon trail as soon as they cleared the big rocks.

"You seem to have a destination in mind."

"I have. If you look far ahead, you will see more of our night guard. They are waiting for us."

"Where are we all going? Does the Chief know?"

"He will soon enough." They rode at a comfortable pace for the horses, cutting across the prairie at an angle. They camped behind the gentle roll in the land that provided a break from the cold wind.

In the morning the young hunters could see the dark collection of cattle in the distance.

At first they thought they were seeing buffalo but as they drew nearer they could tell that these were not buffalo but the beef cattle of the white men.

Two feathers looked at Growling Bear for an instant of indecision.

"Open the gate and bring out half of them," ordered Growling Bear. Two Feathers hesitated, but then he slowly opened the gate and bravely rode in among the huge beasts. Their horns were intimidating. His instruction was to move out about half of the cattle and then close the gate, but once they started to move they all hurried as if they had one mind and one

240

intention. He panicked and yelled when he saw what was happening. The sound only made them move faster. They surged toward the opening, pushing each other against the fence, dislodging poles and forcing the fence to the ground. Two feathers had to go with them or be trampled.

Once the cattle cleared the confines of the fenced field, they scattered running in every direction. Growling Bear had positioned his young men along a line from the open gate to the route they had ridden across the prairie. The cattle didn't behave the way the buffalo had; they ran wildly between his hunters. Some ran in the direction of the mud bog others headed east running at stampede speed away from the Indians and away from the fenced field that had confined them.

Growling Bear was puzzled. They did not behave the way the horses had either. How does anyone control such animals? Many were headed in the direction that he intended. He signaled and his young hunters closed ranks around them and traveled with them as they ran, until they finally slowed.

*****

Adam and Johnny were on the bluff having a cookie when they saw the dark specks running in the distance. They watched as others followed.

"Look," said Johnny pointing.

"Those are not horses. Could they be buffalo?" Adam asked.

"I think they are not buffalo either, they are our cattle," said Johnny. "I can see their horns."

The two boys scrambled down the bluff yelling at the top of their voices. Adam ran toward their new house and Johnny headed for his dad in their barn.

"Our cows are running everywhere! Quick we have to catch them. They are going to be lost," shouted Adam. Johnny was delivering a similar message to Jed.

"Good job son, go back up and watch where they go," said Jed.

"Thanks Adam, I wonder what scared them enough to break out. Tell Sarah and David and find Josh and have them all come, then go back up and keep track of as many as you can and watch where they go," instructed Ben.

"Alright Dad, I will, right away."

Soon the boys were back at the lookout, wishing they were old enough to help with rounding up the cattle. Sarah was the last to cross the river. She had been busy mixing dough and it had taken a couple minutes to get it off her hands and back in the bowl where it would raise.

When she saw the others far out ahead of her she urged Moon Boy to run.

"Ben, how could this happen?" She asked the question as soon as she pulled up and rode next to him.

"I'm not sure Sarah, but thanks for coming to help."

"They seem to be scattered in all directions."

"Look over there. I see some in the trees along the river," said Jed. "Ben I don't see much point in trying to get these animals back where they came from until we see what condition it is in and do what repair is needed."

"You're right. I am going back and get the wagon and a bail of wire and the tools we will need. It won't hurt to head them gently back in that direction, so they don't go farther away."

242

Ben turned Sundown around and headed back to the crossing. I should have done this before I ever headed across the river. He was feeling unsettled and deep inside he was sure this was a manmade problem. He just didn't know yet that it had been Indians.

By the time that Sarah, David, Jed and Joshua had ridden down to Mary's land, they had already come to the right conclusion. Someone had let the cattle out deliberately. There was no obvious sign of who had done it, but Jed had a feeling. He saw the gate standing wide open and several posts broken off and the fence pushed down flat.

"They opened the gate and drove them out. Over here are horse prints, lots of them and they are without shoes. That means one thing to me."

"What are you thinking Jed," asked David. "I think it was the Indians. Father Bob told us that they are badly in need of meat for this winter. They blame the white man for killing the buffalo and driving away the game from their land. It stands to reason that if he mentioned cattle at all when he got back that would start some of the Indians thinking. I'm sure that some of them must have seen Mary's herd when they were out hunting. They probably feel that they have a right to take them, because it's our fault that the animals they need are not here."

"You may be right Jed, but I don't think that Chief Dark Wolf would have sanctioned such a rash action. He doesn't want war."

Ben pulled the wagon up near the broken fence and jumped down.

"Let's try to get this fixed as soon as possible." I brought the last of the posts that we had piled near your barn. I guessed that they would be needed."

"Ben it looks like it was done by the Indians. I noticed lots of horse prints with no shoes. That makes perfect sense. I was fairly certain that it was them. Father Bob told us how much they needed the meat for winter."

"Dad that doesn't matter; they shouldn't steal our cattle."

"Josh I think that they feel it is an appropriate exchange for the animals they used to have. It's not right for them to take them but it isn't right for the white men to shoot the buffalo just for sport and leave them to rot, or they take their hides to sell and the meat is left to waste while the Indians starve. There is no easy answer, but I can tell you this, I am not going to the fort to report this. I don't want men killed over our missing cattle."

"Dad?"

"What Josh?"

"Aren't you going to do anything?"

"Right now I am going to fix this fence and get as many cattle back in here as we can. When that is done, I am going to pray about it and I hope that I can discern God's will in this matter."

"I think we should chase them and make them bring our cattle back."

"How do you think we should do that?"

"I don't know but it seems wrong to just let them get away with it."

"Someone please bring me a new post," said Ben. It took several hours to secure the fence and repair it. Jed and Josh found three of the cattle stuck in the edge of the mud bog. It took some serious maneuvering to get them out unharmed.

"I'm glad you used Big Boy to bring the wagon down. Without his strength I doubt if we could have pulled them out," said Jed.

"That's true, but it would have helped if we were better at roping," he said it with a little laugh. "That's a skill we should all work on." They were able to laugh at their own short comings now that some sense of being in control of the situation was returning. It was true that they could see cattle scattered over the prairie, but Ben was beginning to realize that what he saw was far short of the number that had been there. He had calculated that the Indians had managed to take more than two dozen.

Let's all ride down the middle until we get passed them. We should be able to turn them back toward the hickory and the field. I've got all the gates open and with the wagon across the path by the river they should be inclined to go in their familiar territory. It was a good idea to spread some bundles of winter feed, in there along the back wall. That will coax them in there, too. Once we are down there, we have got to move really slowly. We don't want to start them running again."

"Dad, how many did you count?"

"I'm not sure but I think we have about fifty nine. Let's go home and we can search for more tomorrow. Our guys at the lookout may have a few spotted for us. They filled the water pond and hooked Big Boy up to the wagon and headed back to the ranch.

When Ben entered the house he was wearing a deep furrow on his brow.

"Hi Honey, I think it is time that we went out of the cattle business. I counted as they milled around but I think we caught fifty nine or sixty. They took at least two dozen. There are a few out on the prairie yet. We plan to try to catch them in the morning, if we can."

"Adam, did you and Johnny see many strays down this far?"

"Not really, but I think there are a few in the trees down along the river."

Joshua slid onto his usual spot on one of the benches at the table and wanted to know what they were going to do about the Indian's taking their cattle.

"Josh, I should have known better than to put that herd on the prairie side of the river. It is as much my fault as theirs. You heard what Father Bob said about the Indians needing meat. It's true they are learning about God and the Ten Commandments, but they are baby Christians and they are not going to stay peaceful while their families starve. They blame all white men for the absence of the animals that they hunted just a few years ago."

After a fine meal of fried rabbit, fresh baked bread and garden vegetables, Ben reached for his father's Bible.

"I hope you will all forgive me, Mary, boys, but I need some quiet time with the Lord. I am going down to the hut. Don't wait up for me. Thanks for having the meal ready, Honey. Goodnight." Adam's eyes grew large as his father left the house and they heard him ride down the path.

"Mom, is Dad mad or sad? He had a strange look on his face when he left."

"I think he is troubled. He will read and pray in the hut, and I know that God will help him to know what we are supposed to do."

By the time Ben lit the small fire inside the hut and lit the lantern, he was already feeling that he had done the right thing by coming there. As he knelt he ran his hand over the finely sanded pine floor that he and Jed had put down. He smiled, remembering how excited Mary had been when it was finished.

"Father, I didn't come down here to think about the floor, I am sure you know why I need to talk to you. Mary and I hoped that the cattle would be the start of a legacy for Josh and Adam. I am pretty sure, after today, that it isn't what you had in mind. You gave us gold. Father Bob knows exactly what he should do with his. What are we supposed to do with what Sarah found? You make it clear in your word, that we are to tithe the first fruits of all you give us, crops, cattle, land, and gold, too. I know we must honor that. We want to do it. I am just not sure how you want us to do it. It is a matter of stewardship. Isn't it?"

He opened to Psalm 24 : 1 NIV "The earth is the Lord's and everything in it, the world and all who live in it;" Then Ben turned to Psalm 50:10 NIV "for every animal of the forest is mine and the cattle on a thousand hills."

"That's it! That's what I knew all along. You put these things here for us to use, but not all for our family. We need to use them to help your children. The world belongs to you and all the things in it. Show me Lord how I should proceed, so they will see that the help comes from you." Ben stayed at the hut, praying long into the night. A gentle peace settled on him and when he opened his eyes in the morning, he was sleeping on the bare wood floor without any of the usual comforts. He felt rested and knew that God had everything under control. Ben had his answer.

At the house Mary assured him that the cows were being milked and that Johnny had volunteered to take care of the chickens.

"Adam is at the lookout and Sarah and David have gone to scout out the location of any lost cattle. Beth is bringing Lily down to spend the day here so she can work in the garden. After the milking, Jed and Josh will come down and you three can go see if you can round up any more of the cattle."

"Just as I thought, everything is under control," he said with a smile.

*****

Two Feathers began to worry as they traveled along with the cattle. This is wrong, he thought. This will bring trouble to the camp of the Blue Stone People. He looked at the wide trail they were leaving in the prairie grass. Anyone could follow the tracks these heavy beasts leave. I wish I had not taken part in this. Willow will be disappointed in me and Chief Dark Wolf will be furious with all of us. I should not have listened to Growling Bear. This was his idea. The man that owns these cattle is sure to be angry and he will report it. If the soldiers come, many of the people will be killed.

Two Feathers regretted his role in this, more than anything he had ever done.

When he looked up, he saw a single rider coming. It was Father Bob.

Father Bob had talked with the Chief about acquiring beef for the people. He was on his way to the S. and J. Ranch to buy some cattle.

When he realized that the men from the village were bringing cattle, he instantly knew that they had stolen them.

Growling Bear pulled his horse up and stopped, motioning for the rest of them to continue on.

"Growling Bear, what have you done?"

"Hello, Father Bob," he said with a wide smile. "We are bringing meat for the people."

"Did you trade for the cattle?"

"We took what they have taken from us. They have taken away the deer and the buffalo. That was our meat, until they came with their fences. Now we take the meat that our people need for winter."

"Oh Growling Bear, this is not the way to get meat. You have taken our peace and have opened the door for war. The Great Spirit says you must not steal. He will not bless the people if you do not honor His rules."

"You are soft, Priest. We do what we must." He kicked his horse and rode swiftly around the herd disturbing them.

When he reached the guard at the opening to the big rocks path, he ordered the man on guard to ride through and open the gate to the meadow.

As the big rocks loomed ahead, the cattle slowed and stopped moving forward. They began to mill around, uncertain of the path.

"Two Feathers ride through and show them the way," signed Growling Bear.

Two Feathers moved slowly to the front of the small herd of cattle and walked his horse in the opening of the path. When he looked back he was astonished that it had actually worked. The cattle were following! The night guards stayed close gently pressing them to the opening.

Chief Dark Wolf was shocked when he saw the first few cattle enter the meadow.

As more came in, his face began to display his disbelief. How could they be so senseless? This is going to cause trouble. At first he had seen Two Feathers come through the path in front of the cattle. At that moment he thought that this was his doing but he knew differently when Growling Bear proudly entered the meadow last, following the men of the night guard that he had taken. The man on guard closed the gate noticing that the horses had all gone to the far end of the field. Coyote and Falling Stones were concerned. They feared that the big horned beasts would injure the horses.

Chief Dark Wolf knew that it was far too soon for Father Bob to have arranged the purchase of cattle for the people.

"White Grass, tell Growling Bear that I want to see him now!"

"Yes my Chief."

White Grass hurried along the outside of the meadow motioning to Growling Bear.

"The Chief is in his tent. He wants to see you right away," said the young man.

Growling Bear glanced in that direction and saw Moonflower scurry away from the front of her tent when her husband approached. Behind him in the meadow she could see the cattle. He had turned and sent White Grass dashing to deliver a message. The look on his face was enough to tell her that she did not want to be here just now. He didn't have to tell her.

Morning Dove stood outside her tent with Roaring Water her husband. Moonflower joined them.

"The Priest has not had time to go purchase these animals. Growling Bear has brought us meat but with it I fear he has brought death to this camp. I am going to talk to some of the other hunters. Chief Dark wolf will call a meeting in the big tent soon. He will want us to be ready to defend the camp," said Roaring Water.

He walked toward the edge of the big rocks where Night Hawk and Snapping Turtle stood talking animatedly.

Growling Bear responded to the summons joyously. He was not thinking clearly. He expected praise.

When he scratched on the tent flap of Chief Dark Wolf, he was not ready for the shout that met his arrival.

"Growling Bear, you are a fool! This will bring the soldiers here for the first time! I can't believe that you think that this is the way to feed our people. Have you lived here with us and not learned the moral code of our people? We do not steal! You have taken the lives of our people in your hands and their blood will pour over you!"

Growling Bear stood silently. He did not respond. I had to get meat, he thought. He only half heard the words the Chief was saying. He felt anger wash over him.

"Is this how you thank me for bringing food for all our people to last the winter? I have taken back what they took from us! They took the buffalo and the deer!"

He was shouting, and Chief Dark Wolf couldn't believe that even now, Growling Bear could not see the harm in what he had done.

"Who gave you permission to leave our camp unguarded?

Who said you could take the night guard and leave camp? Are you now an authority here that answers to no one? Growling Bear this was wrong on so many levels that I can't begin to explain it. If you can't see it, then you are no longer capable of being my top hunter and warrior. Your skills have always been a strength that I could count on, but now I cannot believe the decision you have made! Go to your tent and stay there until I send for you. Do not leave your tent! Do you understand?"

"Yes my Chief," he said humbly as he backed out the flap and went to his own tent swiftly. He knew their words had boomed over the immediate area.

As tongues wagged; everyone would know his disgrace in a few minutes. He wondered how he could survive this humiliation. His anger boiled on top of his crushed spirit. For the very first time since he had become leader of the warriors and hunters, he felt that the Chief no longer had respect for him.

Big Flower had watched him enter the meadow with the cattle and then she observed as he went to the Chief's tent. She was aware of the concern that he had caused by taking the night guard without telling Chief Dark Wolf. She thought that was the issue at hand. She didn't realize that he had stolen the cattle and the possibility loomed that soldiers would follow.

Her first instinct was to try to comfort him, but when she saw the blood red of his angry face, she darted out and went to the shade pavilion where her children were.

*****

Father Bob stood on the prairie not sure what he should do now that Growling Bear had ruined his plan to purchase some cattle. I need to get to Ben before he goes to the fort.

"Father God, please help me to handle this the right way." He slid back up on Macho and headed for the Hickory. He stopped once and took a drink from his water bag and offered Macho a drink from a woven basket that had been waterproof at one time, but now it dripped a steady stream as the horse drank. I probably should not have folded that and stuffed it in my saddlebag. I broke the weaving.

He was determined to keep his promise to always take good care of Macho. He sat in the middle of the prairie grass and prayed, asking God to keep Ben busy long enough for him to reach the ranch before he left for the fort. God you are the father of the Blue Stone People. We both know that Growling Bear is a hard sell when it comes to teaching him about your son Jesus, but I know that your commandments are written on his heart. Help him to accept that you are their provision and that you will take care of your children.

"Macho, are you ready? Let's go my friend. He swung up and once again they headed for the river and the big oak that marked the crossing. Macho was very tired and Father Bob was delighted when they reached the crossing. Ben and Jed were there to greet him. They had returned from gathering the strays an hour earlier.

"I rode all night Ben. I did stop once for Macho, but he is exhausted. I am tired too, but I had to see if I could get here before you went to the fort. Ben and Jed, I am so sorry. Chief Dark Wolf did not tell them to take the cattle and I know he does not approve. I am sure that they are in big trouble with him. He had just given me blue stones and permission to come to your ranch to see if you would help us get some cattle to the people."

He was talking fast and his strained emotion was apparent.

The three men walked up the path to Jed's house. Jed took Macho and put him in his corral. Ben and Father Bob waited on the steps for him to join them. They went in together.

"Welcome Father Bob. I am surprised to see you again so soon," said Beth. Please sit down at the table. She poured them all tea and put a plate of cookies nearby.

"Beth, I didn't know that I would be back this soon. Chief Dark Wolf has asked me to come see if Ben would sell some of your beef cattle so the people won't go hungry this winter. He did not sanction the raid on your cattle and in fact they were acting on their own and he had no knowledge of it. Ben, please don't involve the soldiers. I will pay top dollar to you right now, and I will give you extra to pay for the fence or anything they damaged. Words fail me. Chief Dark Wolf had already sent me on my way when I met the men coming with the cattle. You take whatever you think is a fair price."

He poured the many large pieces of turquoise onto the table from an intricately beaded leather pouch.

"Father, I am not intending to go to the fort. You can be assured of that. Relax and I am guessing you are hungry. Beth, give Father Bob some of that nice stew you made."

"No thanks, I don't want to cause any of you any more trouble than you have already had. Please just tell me that you accept the apology and will take payment for the cattle."

"Father Bob, you can't pay us for the cattle. It is too late." Ben paused, walking over to the stove and filling his cup.

"I spent the night with the Lord, and I admit that I was pretty angry when we first discovered what they had done, but God reminded me in Psalm 50:10 that every animal of the forest is His, and He owns the cattle on a thousand hills, and that includes the ones the Indians took. How thoughtless and irresponsible would we all be, if we kept all that beef penned up here, while People of the Blue Stone Camp were going hungry? I am not sure what God intended, for us to do to get the cattle to them, but hopefully they have enough now to get them through this winter. I am going to make some arrangements so they have a supply they can count on. I think the Blue Stone hunters are going to have to become wranglers.

Father Bob was stunned. He had not expected to find Ben in an understanding frame of mind. He was amazed and speechless. He wrapped his arms around Ben and wept uncontrollably.

"Thank you Ben. Thank you to all of you," he managed to say after a few moments. He wiped his eyes and sat back down.

"Now will you have something to eat?" Beth asked as she poured him a cup of freshly made coffee. "Let's all relax. We can talk about this and solve the logistics of it in the morning.

*****

All the men of the S. and J. Ranch gathered for the meeting in Jed's barn as soon as the morning chores were finished. Adam and Johnny were included, but unlike the Blue Stone People, they soon found that their meeting included women and children. Sarah came in right behind David and Mary brought the wagon with Eli and Natty. Beth walked to the barn with Lily and soon everyone was talking to Father Bob at once.

"Stop," said Ben. "No one can understand what is being said. Let's do this with some order," he smiled but his tone was serious.

"We have two issues that need to be handled. The first is that we need to strip the visible gold from the river on our properties. Does anyone have a suggestion?"

"I do," said Mary. "We are all used to working on projects together. Let's make lots of big sacks and put them on the wagon. Then we can go down to David's land and start on the up-river side and pick rocks until we can't find a sparkle. We can keep going and do the same for Father Bob's."

"Of course we do need to remove the surface gold, but once it is taken from the river, where will we put it?"

"Ben, I think you and Jed need to prepare to bury a couple more horses," said Mary.

"What are you talking about woman?" asked Jed.

"David was laughing. I know what she is talking about. You are right Mary. We can dig a cache back

256

where we buried the old horse and put the gold in it. Anyone that visits would never see the caches. We can put thick sod on the top where it opens."

"We shouldn't keep going down there on the prairie side. It would be better to cross somewhere else and use the back side of the river to pull the gold out."

"Josh, that's a good suggestion."

Father Bob said he would leave in the morning and come back as soon as possible with a borrowed pair of the big work horses from the herd of the people. "I will use them to pull stumps and that will create a visual activity that will explain any change in that area. I am certain that God put the gold there as a provision for the people. It will pay for the cattle and a mission."

"I would like to move the visible gold before the first snow," answered Ben. "The river gets very cold this time of year. "How long will it take us to make two big caches?"

"Not very long, maybe a couple days," said David, "It might be better to go gather the gold first and then we will know how big they need to be."

"Should we have the rocks tested? We could all be getting excited about fool's gold," said Beth. "This could all be a lot of hard work for nothing."

"Beth, I don't know if there is an assayer's office in Silverville now. Things are changing so fast. There could be, but if we took gold in there and had it tested, the entire Hickory would be crawling with people looking for gold.

*****

The next day was one of the days that the soldiers came to collect milk, butter, cheese and eggs from the ranch. They brought with them a newspaper.

257

A new resident had set up an office and was now printing a paper once a week. He also told them that the mail was now brought down the Silver and left at the Trading Post. They would have regular delivery and pick up now, once a week.

Suddenly Ben realized that he would be able to send a letter to the family they had left behind. He wondered how many of them would still be there to read it.

As he gazed at the one sheet newspaper, he noticed an advertisement down in the corner. He read the words "Gold Assayer's Kit, by mail. The price was one dollar.

"That's a lot of money, but I think Josh would have a lot of fun with that. I think I will send for it for his birthday," he told the soldier.

"He is a nice lad. He seems responsible enough to have something like that," said the soldier. "We all wish that we had real gold to test," he said with a little laugh. "You can keep the paper. I have read it all several times."

He slowly turned the wagon around. The milk and other goods were packed in tight, and blocks of ice kept it cold. Bundles of hay kept it steady and insulated too.

"I almost forgot to tell you. The Major said that last batch of cheese was the best he had ever had."

"I'll be sure to tell Beth. She will be pleased."

As the soldier pulled away, Ben was already pondering how he could write a letter to his family back home. I need to fill in the years that we have all been separated. He wondered who was left to read it. I was fifteen and I'm going to be twenty nine this fall. All my cousins are grown and probably married. They will be

258

sad when I tell them about Father and Mother and the way they were killed. They will all be amazed when I tell them that I married a woman with two sons and now we have four! I can tell them that Sarah is here and married and happy. That's all they need to know this first letter. I am eager for a reply and I haven't sent it yet. He laughed at his excitement. I know it will probably take a great deal of time to get there, but at least it is possible now. I can't wait to tell everyone. We are starting a new chapter in our lives!

Adam and Johnny had watched the wagon pull slowly away and then scurried down to see what Ben was holding in his hands.

"I have something to tell everyone. Spread the news, boys, and I will be waiting in my house." Adam headed for Sarah's and Johnny ran to find his father and mother. It took a few minutes to get everyone there. Josh rode out to the field where David was working.

"Is something wrong?"

"No I don't think so," he said "but you should come now." David nodded and swung up on Blackie.

"Let's go," he said and they galloped to the far gate near Ben's new house.

Inside, they could hear everyone talking at once.

"It sounds like a gaggle of geese," said David. Josh laughed, but he had never heard geese. He could only imagine.

Sarah was in the kitchen with Mary.

"This should help a lot. I don't know what I ate to upset my stomach, but it has been bothering me the last two days." Sarah sipped the mint and ginger tea and waited for Ben to tell them his news.

"Ben, we are all waiting. What are you smiling about?"

Jed asked impatiently as David and Josh stepped in the front door.

"The first thing is this!" He held out the paper for them to see. There is a newspaper being printed right in Silverville. This is a copy of the first paper!"

"Wow, that's great," said Josh. Everyone will know what is happening now." They all gathered close to look at it.

"Look down there." He pointed at the small advertisement in the corner. "We can get an assaying kit for testing gold right in the mail. Here's the best part of all! The mail comes down to the trading post and we can send and receive mail. So much is changing. We have many things to work on. I need to arrange for the cattle on a regular basis for the Blue Stone People. Father Bob will be back with the work horses to pull stumps and we have gold to gather and two caches to dig. I have a letter to write and that gold testing kit to order. We all have God's work to do.

AN INVITATION

If you do not know Jesus, as your savior, but you would like Him to be, please pray the following prayer. Invite Him into your heart. Commit your "New Life" to Him. He will be your constant companion, counselor, comforter, and protector. The Holy Bible tells us that He will never leave you or forsake you.

"Dear Jesus, please forgive my sins. Give me grace Lord, so that I will not commit them again. Come into my heart and strengthen me, so that I can start a "New Life" with you as my companion. I want to live according to your will and commandments. Bless me Lord and lead me in a life that is pleasing to you. In Jesus' Holy name I pray. Amen"

If you prayed that prayer, you are saved. You are born again. Your soul is whiter than the snow on the highest mountains. The angels in heaven are rejoicing as they write your name in The Lamb's Book of Life.

Get a Holy Bible and begin to read it. Find a good Bible believing church and start attending, so that you can learn more about Your Heavenly Father. Jesus said that we should be baptized and filled with his Holy Spirit. What a wonderful God we have.

If you wish, you can sign and date your Bible as an outward sign that you have committed your life to Christ. Tell someone that you have a new life in Christ.

I will pray for you. God bless you. Louise Bouck

Book Titles in this New Life Series

Book #1 More Than Survival
Book #2 Life's Many Journeys
Book #3 The Land's Heritage
Book #4 The Story of Sarah
Book #5 Together
Book #6 The Blue Stone People
Book #7 Teewahpanyee The Boy, Two Feathers The Man
Book #8 The People of the Lion
Book #9 The Lion's Den
Book #10 Just The Beginning

www.ingramcontent.com/pod-product-compliance
Lightning Source LLC
Chambersburg PA
CBHW050725180626

46814CB00002B/605